Their Amish Reunion

Lenora Worth

D0126592

H HARLEQUIN® LOVE INSPIRED®

Recycling programs for this product may not exist in your area.

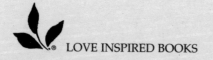

LOVE INSPIRED BOOKS

ISBN-13: 978-1-335-42798-4

Their Amish Reunion

Copyright © 2018 by Lenora H. Nazworth

www.Harlequin.com

Printed in U.S.A.

"And ye shall seek me, and find me, when ye shall search for me with all your heart."
—*Jeremiah* 29:13

To Marta Perry, a mentor and friend
and incredible writer.

Thank you, Marta,
for your encouragement and support.

Chapter One

He thought of Ava Jane.

The memory of her sweet smile had held him together for so long, Jeremiah wondered if he'd ever be able to face her again. The real *her*. The one he'd left behind. Remembering her pretty smile was one thing. Coming face-to-face with her and seeing the hurt and condemnation in her eyes would be another.

Something he'd dreaded during the long bus trip across the country from California to Pennsylvania.

But he wasn't here today to meet with the bishop about Ava Jane. He'd lost her and he'd accepted that long ago. He didn't deserve her anymore. Twelve years was a long time. She'd made a good life with a good man. Or so he'd heard.

She had not waited for Jeremiah to come

home because all indications had shown he never would come home again. At times, he'd thought that same thing. Thought he was surely going to die a world away from the one he'd left. At those times, he'd think of her rich strawberry blonde curls and her light-as-air blue eyes. And her wide, glowing smile. And he'd wish he'd never left her.

But he was here now, waiting inside the bishop's home to speak to him. Here and needing to find some solace. He came back to help his family, whether they wanted him to or not. His younger sister, Beth, had tried to keep in touch, but her last letter had been full of fear and grief.

"Daed is dying, Jeremiah. Please come quickly."

Bishop King walked into the sparsely decorated parlor where Jeremiah waited and stood for a moment. The man's gaze was solemn and unreadable, but his dark eyes held a glimmer of hope.

"Young Jeremiah Weaver," the bishop said before he took his time settling down in a high-back walnut chair across from Jeremiah. "Have you *kumm* back to your faith?"

Jeremiah held his head down and studied his hands, horrible memories of rapid gunfire and grown men moaning in pain filling his brain. Studied his hands and wished he could change them, take away the scars and calluses of war and replace them with the blisters and calluses of good, honest work.

He needed to find some peace.

That was why he'd come home to Lancaster County and his Amish roots. So he looked the bishop in the eyes and nodded.

"*Ja*, Bishop King, I've *kumm* home. For *gut*."

Home for good. One of the hardest things he'd ever had to do in his life. Because the hardest thing he'd ever done was leave Ava Jane crying in the dark.

Ava Jane Graber grabbed her ten-year-old son, Eli, by the collar of his shirt and shook her head. "Eli, please stop picking up things, *alleweil*." Right now. "You might break something."

"Sorry, Mamm," Eli replied, his mischievous brown eyes reminding her of her late husband, Jacob.

Jacob had drowned two years ago while trying to save a calf during a storm, but he used to love teasing her. Eli had inherited his father's gift of mirth and his gift of getting into trouble.

Sarah Rose, soon turning seven, seemed to have Ava Jane's sensibilities and logical nature. Her blue eyes grew as she twisted her brow. "Eli, you know Mamm doesn't like it when we break things." Putting her little hands on her hips, the child added, "And you break things all the time."

Hmm. Her young daughter could also be a tad judgmental at times. Had she also inherited that from Ava Jane?

Ava Jane shook her head and gathered the few supplies she'd come into town to buy. "No, Mamm does not like it when you misbehave and accidentally break things."

Smiling at Mr. Hartford, the general store owner, she paid for her items and said, *"Denke."*

"You're welcome, Ava Jane, and thank you for the fresh apple muffins," the Englisch manager said with a wide grin. "Good to see you out and about today."

"It's a fine spring morning," Ava Jane replied, her items and her children in tow. Mr. Hartford loved it when she brought him fresh baked goods to sell, but he also liked that she saved a couple of choices just for him. "A wonderful, beautiful day."

"One of the Lord's best," Mr. Hartford said with a nod.

But when she walked out onto the sidewalk toward her waiting horse and buggy, her beautiful morning turned into something she couldn't explain.

She looked up and into the deep blue eyes of the man walking toward them, her bag of groceries slipping right out of her grip. The paper bag tore and all her purchases crashed down, the sound of shattering glass echoing off the pavement.

"I think Mamm just broke something," Eli pointed out, his gaze moving from her to the hard-edged man wearing a T-shirt and jeans, his dark hair curling around his face and neck.

"Who is that, Mamm?" Sarah Rose asked, her distinctive intuition shining brightly as her gaze moved from Ava Jane to the man.

Ava Jane couldn't speak, couldn't elaborate. But inside, she was shouting and screaming and wishing she could take her children and run away. Her heart had shattered right along with the jar of fresh honey she'd purchased.

She knew this man. Had thought about him time and again over the years.

Jeremiah Weaver.

The man who'd left her behind.

Jeremiah couldn't stop himself. He rushed toward Ava Jane and the *kinder* with all the might he'd used to charge against the enemy while wearing heavy tactical gear.

"Ava Jane?" he called, fearful that she was going to pass out. Her skin, always as fresh as new peaches, turned pale, her sky blue eyes filled with shock, the pupils dilating.

He'd startled her. He had not meant to let her see him this way, here on the street in the small town of Campton Creek, where everyone talked too much about things of which they knew nothing. Wishing he'd had more time to prepare, Jeremiah couldn't hide from her now.

"Ava Jane?" he said again when he'd made it to her side. "Are you all right?"

"Was denkscht?" she asked, anger in the phrase, her heart-shaped face dark with confusion.

What do you think?

Jeremiah saw a bench. *"Kumm,* sit."

"Mamm?" the little girl said on a wail, fright clear in her eyes. "May we go home?"

Ava Jane looked from her confused daughter back to Jeremiah. "In a minute, Sarah Rose. Go with your brother to the buggy and wait for me."

"You made a mess," the boy pointed out, love for his *mamm* shining in his eyes. "I can clean it for you."

Jeremiah could see Jacob in the boy's eyes. Jacob, one of his best friends. Married to the woman he'd loved.

"I'll clean it up in a bit," Jeremiah offered, taking Ava Jane by the arm to guide her to the bench. Few people were out and about but those who were, including some Amish, had stopped to stare.

She pulled away. "I'll get Mr. Hartford. Go now, Eli, and wait by the horses."

The *kinder* did as she requested. Only when they were out of earshot did she turn back to him, her eyes blazing like a hot sky. "What are you doing here, Jeremiah?"

"I didn't want you to see me yet," he tried to explain.

"Too late." She adjusted her white *kapp* with shaking hands. "I need to go."

"Please don't," he said. "I'm not going to bother you. I... I saw you and I didn't have time to—"

"To leave again?" she asked, her tone full of more venom than he could ever imagine coming from such a sweet soul.

"I'm not leaving," he said. "I'm here to stay. I've come back to Campton Creek to help my family. But I had planned on coming to pay you and Jacob a visit, to let you know that... I understand how things are now. You're married—"

"I'm a widow now," she blurted, two bright spots forming on her cheeks. "And I have to get my children home."

Kneeling, she tried to pick up her groceries but his hand on her arm stopped her. Jeremiah took the torn bag and placed the thread, spices and canned goods at the bottom, the feel of sticky honey on his fingers merging with the memory of her dainty arm. But the shock of her words made him numb with regret.

I'm a widow now.

"I'm sorry," Jeremiah said in a whisper. "Beth never told me."

"You couldn't be reached."

Ah, so Beth had tried but he'd been on a mission.

"I wish I'd known. I'm so sorry."

Ava Jane kept her eyes downcast while she tried to gather the rest of her groceries and toss them in the torn bag.

"Here you go," he said, the bag tightly rolled while her news echoed through his mind and left him stunned. "I'll go inside and get something to clean the honey."

Their eyes met while his hand brushed over hers.

A rush of deep longing shot through her eyes, jagged and fractured, and hit Jeremiah straight in his heart.

Ava Jane recoiled and stood. *"Denke."*

Then she turned and hurried toward the buggy. Just before she lifted her skirts to get inside, she pivoted back to give him one last glaring appraisal. "I wonder why you came back at all."

He watched as she got in the buggy and sat for a moment before she gave the reins to her son. Without a backward glance, Ava Jane held her head high. Then Jeremiah hurried into Hartford's and asked for a wet mop to clean the stains from the sidewalk. He only wished he could clean away the stains inside of his heart.

And just like her, he wondered why he'd returned to Campton Creek.

Ava Jane didn't know how she'd made it the two miles home. She'd been so shaken that she'd allowed Eli to guide the buggy. Knowing that their docile roan mare, Matilda, would get them home safely, Ava Jane watched her son handling the reins, her sight blurred by an ache that caught her at the oddest of times.

Well, seeing Jeremiah in *Englisch* clothes had certainly been odd. Seeing him, his blue-black eyes holding hers, so many unspoken things between them, had certainly been confusing and overwhelming. His hand brushing against hers had brought back memories of how they used to hold hands and sneak chaste kisses. She felt a headache coming on.

Why was he back?

Twelve years had passed since he'd awakened her in the middle of the night and asked her to come out onto the porch between the main house and the *grossdaadi haus* where her grandparents lived.

Twelve years since Jeremiah had taken his *rumspringa* to a whole new level while she'd barely done anything different during her own. Her heart was here in Campton Creek while his heart had longed for adventure and…war.

War. He'd become a warrior, hardened and battle scarred and unyielding. A Navy warrior. SEALs, they called themselves. In desperation, she'd gone to the library and found all kinds of articles that explained things much too clearly to her. He'd gone against the Amish way and joined the military.

What had he done and seen out there?

"I have to go, Ava Jane," he said that night so long ago, tears in his eyes. "I can't explain it but…something has happened. Something bad."

"Was ist letz?" she asked, her heart pumping too fast. "What's the matter?"

"Edward is dead."

She knew Edward Campton, ten years older at the time than Jeremiah's seventeen. He and Jeremiah became good friends when Mr. Weaver and Jeremiah went to the stately Campton mansion centered in the heart of Campton Creek to build some new cabinets in the kitchen. Edward, a Navy SEAL, was home on leave for a couple of months and, for some reason, he'd told Jeremiah things he wasn't supposed to tell anyone.

But then, Jeremiah always had a rough streak.

He loved to wrestle and fight, to swim as fast as he could, to be the first to win in any game. And he often talked about things of the world, hunting and fishing, which the Amish did only for food. Jeremiah became fascinated with battles and war games and sailing the open seas, things their kind did not condone.

During his second year of *rumspringa*, the time all Amish teens and young adults had a chance to run around before they settled down and became baptized, Jeremiah became enamored of Edward. Edward's Englisch ways and military talk swayed Jeremiah and changed him. Soon, Jeremiah began to spend more and more time with Edward, running and exercising with him, swimming in the big pool behind the Campton mansion, learning all about dangerous weapons and listening to Edward's stories of valor. Even learning how to scuba dive, of all things.

Edward loaned him history books full of stories of valor, which Jeremiah read late at night after his chores were done. After he came by to see her and tell her he loved her which he often did back then.

Why, she'd never understand. *Why, Jeremiah?* Why had he felt the need to run away and join the Navy?

She heard talk in town about the Campton

family. Their roots stretched back to the American Revolution and the town was named for them. They were rich and had a house full of material things. The minute Jeremiah met Edward, she'd felt him slipping away from her. All his talk about history and battles and honoring the country that protected and sheltered him.

He'd been almost eighteen and able to make his own decisions. Finally, he'd told her he wasn't sure he wanted to be baptized. He wasn't sure he wanted to stay Amish. Jeremiah had always been adventurous and he'd often talked about things of the world, but he changed right before her eyes. She saw the change the last time they'd talked.

"Jeremiah, what are you saying? Your place is here, with me. This is our life. The life God gave us."

But that night she'd lost him completely. His friend who'd gone back to his duties had been on a dangerous mission to find and kill a known terrorist, he explained.

"I was at the Campton place a few hours ago, helping Mr. Campton with replacing some worn floors. They were watching a news report on television about a secretive raid that happened a few days ago. I could tell they were concerned. Then these two men in uniform showed up at the door. Mrs. Campton screamed out and we ran to her. Mr. Campton saw the two men and started to cry. It was horrible. They'd come to tell them that Edward was dead. Killed in the raid. Killed, Ava Jane."

Once Ava Jane heard that and after Jeremiah told her he'd been there when they'd received the terrible news, she knew she'd lost Jeremiah.

His friend who'd served his country as a Navy SEAL had died, and now Jeremiah wanted to join up and fight an unspeakable enemy to avenge that death. That went against the tenets of their faith.

"No, Jeremiah, no," she cried. "I beg you, don't do this. We don't get involved in these things. We don't fight wars. Stay with me. We have plans, remember? Our own home, children. A life together. We've talked about it since we were thirteen."

"I want that life," he said, tears streaming down his face. "But I have to do this now, while I'm young. I'll come back one day. Soon." His hands on her face, he looked into her eyes, torment twisting his expression. "I can't explain it, but I have to go."

"No." She didn't agree with him, did not agree with how he followed Edward around, always asking questions and trying to be Englisch. He'd spent his *rumspringa* trying to be someone he wasn't and now he'd become someone she didn't know.

Blinking away tears, she came back to the present, focused on her children and tried to take a breath.

But he's back.

He'd said he'd come home to help his family. True, his *daed* was ill, first from a broken hip and now with an infection that wouldn't heal. After many weeks in a nearby hospital, Isaac had requested he be brought home. He now lay, in and out of consciousness. It was just a matter of time.

But who had summoned Jeremiah home?

Surely not his stubborn, hard *daed*, who'd banned Jeremiah from their home. Probably not his *mamm*. She'd never go against her husband's wishes. Probably his sister, Beth.

The siblings had managed to stay close through the years. Beth often gave Ava Jane updates, even when she'd never asked for them. Sometimes, he couldn't be located, such as when Jacob had died. His life had become so secretive and covert. Because it had become a dangerous life. Ava Jane had prayed for Jeremiah so many times. That was her duty. She prayed for everyone she knew. But she'd never prayed him home. Not once.

She wanted no part of the man.

She wanted to go back to that night and hear him say instead, "I'll stay, Ava Jane. For you. Only you."

Stop it, she told herself. *Think of Jacob. You can have no betrayal of your husband in your thoughts.*

So now while her children did their chores and ran around in the sunshine, chasing butterflies, Ava Jane sat in Jacob's rocking chair and cried for her husband, her head pounding with both physical and mental pain. She needed his warmth right now. She needed him here with her in their safe, comfortable beloved world. Jacob would hold her close and tell her he'd protect her and take care of her. No matter what.

Her husband had tried to show her the love that Jeremiah had thrown away and, in turn, she'd tried to be a good wife to Jacob. They had truly grown to love each other. They'd been together through the loss of both of Jacob's parents, first his mother and then, a year later, his father. Jacob never quite got over losing his parents. But then he'd died five years later.

Now, struggling on her small farm, she didn't have Jacob to shield her from the pain of seeing Jeremiah again. Jeremiah, the same but so different.

Ava Jane tugged her shawl tightly around her

as the gloaming fell across the green grass and newly budding fruit trees, the last of the sun's rays covering the hills and valleys and rooftops like a light linen veil. She wondered how she'd ever be able to accept Jeremiah being back in Campton Creek. No matter that she was allowed to speak to him since he'd never been baptized and there was no ban on him. No matter that she might not see him every day anyway. No matter that his family needed him and he'd heeded that call. None of it mattered and she shouldn't even fret about these things.

Just knowing he was nearby—that would be the hard thing.

Ava Jane rubbed her aching temples and sipped the tea she hoped would subdue the agony attacking her brain.

Dear Lord, give me the strength to go about my life. He has no meaning to me now. I have to forget he's back.

She would. She'd go on the way she'd been doing. She was blessed and, while she grieved the loss of her husband, she had to consider her children. They had kept her going these past two years. She'd concentrate on them and their needs.

But, even through her fervent prayers, Ava

Jane knew that trying to put Jeremiah Weaver out of her mind would be like trying not to breathe.

Impossible.

Chapter Two

News traveled fast in the Amish community. Jeremiah knew before he approached the dirt lane leading up to his family home that they would be expecting him, even if they probably dreaded him being here. Bishop King had offered to come and talk to them, but Jeremiah wasn't sure if he indeed had made it by yet or how well that visit had gone. Maybe they could all meet with the bishop as a family. The bishop and the ministers had given Jeremiah their blessings to go through the eighteen required weeks of lessons he'd need before he could be baptized.

He'd already started on that at least, and he'd kept in touch with Beth so she'd know he was close by in case his father took a turn for the worse.

"When are you coming home to us?" his sister had asked when he'd sent her word to call him at the Campton estate.

"After I take care of a few things."

Things such as transferring the money he'd saved to a bank here so he could help his family financially and set up provisions for his mother and sister.

He'd wanted to talk to Ava Jane, too, but he'd never found the courage. So now, she knew he was back. Soon the whole community would know he'd returned. He'd stalled long enough.

These last few weeks, he'd been staying in the guesthouse at Campton House and working for the now-elderly Camptons. But after seeing Ava Jane yesterday outside Hartford's General Store, he knew it was time to do what he'd set out to do.

He had to face his family.

Beth had faithfully written to him through the years. That was allowed at least. He knew a lot of Amish who kept in touch with relatives who'd gone out into the Englisch world.

Mamm always sent her love but even now she wouldn't talk to him if his *daed* was alert and aware. But Daed. That was another matter. While he had not officially been shunned since he'd never been baptized, Jeremiah knew he'd been gone a long time. His *daed* had made it clear he was not welcome back in the Weaver house, unless he was willing to give his confession and be baptized. Then Jeremiah would be welcomed back and forgiven, and the past would be the past.

Only, he'd brought his past with him. Not willing to think about that now, he made his way up to the wide, welcoming porch that his *mamm* and sister kept swept and spotless. Already, a riotous bed of flowers bloomed in shades of purple, red and blue all along the porch border. Two potted plants graced each side of the front door. His mother and sister loved their gardens. Daed frowned on such frivolous colors, but Jeremiah knew his father well enough to know Isaac Weaver would do anything to make his wife smile.

Anything but forgive his only son for leaving. His father might accept him back, but Jeremiah wondered if that wound could ever be completely healed. He'd deserted his family.

The bishop had given Jeremiah some advice to help him get started on the process of attending baptism sessions, which happened an hour before church on every other Sunday. Then he needed to get right with his family. The bishop had prayed with him about that, too. And, while Jeremiah had not been ready to share everything he'd seen and done, Bishop King had offered him some hope. "You can talk to me, Jeremiah. Anytime, about anything. *Wilkum* home."

Thankful for that, Jeremiah had asked, "Where do I start?"

Rubbing his silver beard, Bishop King had lowered his head. "Your *daed* is gravely ill. He might not ever know you are home but Isaac will be glad in his heart to see you return. I encourage you to talk to him, even if he seems to be sleeping. Your *mamm* and sister need a strong man about. The place is going down in spite of neighbors pitching in to help. You will step up, Jeremiah. And in time you'll begin to heal."

He was about to step up, all right. He might not be able to truly be a part of this family but he'd do the right thing because he was ready now. Ready to settle down and give his life back to the Lord. Jeremiah would do whatever it took to find his way back to God.

And to Ava Jane.

He hadn't planned on trying to win her back but…she was alone now. She needed him and, even though she'd acted afraid and angry, he'd seen the truth when he'd touched her hand and looked into her eyes. She could love him again with time and forgiveness. Now he had a wonderful reason to work hard to prove his intentions. He'd make things right with God and his family and then he'd win Ava Jane back. It would be the toughest battle of his life.

Now he stood at the steps of the home where he'd been raised, memories coloring his mind in the same way those flowers colored the yard. But the pretty flowers couldn't hide the gloomy facade surrounding the big rectangular two-story house. One of the porch posts needed replacing, and the whole place could use a good coat of paint. The house contained four big bedrooms and a large open kitchen and dining area with a cozy sitting area by the woodstove. Big enough to hold church services, if need be. A large basement for storage and summer use. And the *grossdaadi haus* where his grandparents had lived before their deaths.

A lot needed to be done around here.

Jeremiah closed his eyes and thought about growing up on this vast farm. The laughter, the discussions, the prayers before each meal, the hard work. A heavy mist filled his eyes. He opened them and took a deep breath to calm himself.

Home.

Before he could take another step, his younger sister, Beth, rushed out the door and flung herself into his arms.

"Jeremiah, you're home! *Gott segen eich.*"

God bless you.

Jeremiah held her close, the scent of lavender and fresh soap cleansing away the ugliness of what he'd seen on the battlefield.

He held her for only a second and then stepped back. "Shh, now. You know Daed wouldn't want you touching me."

She blinked back tears, her dark hair spilling around her white *kapp* like smooth chocolate. "Daed doesn't wake up much anymore. We need you home and I need a hug from my big brother, *ja*."

"Where's Mamm?" he asked, his voice clogged with emotion. He smelled pot roast and gravy, maybe even biscuits. His mouth watered just thinking about his mother's cooking.

"Seeing to Daed in the downstairs room," Beth replied. "*Kumm*, we have a grand feast for you."

"A feast for the prodigal?"

Beth gave him a solid stare, her blue eyes bright. "*Ja*. And glad to have him home at that."

Ava Jane sat down next to her sister. Once or twice a week, she and her sister and some other friends got together to quilt and bake, taking turns to host. Some might call this time together a frolic and they did frolic, but they also worked and prayed and shared common joys and concerns.

Her friends had seen her through two babies and the loss of her in-laws and her husband. She loved them dearly and counted her sister, Deborah, as a friend, too. Deborah had been eight years old when Jeremiah had left. Ava Jane remembered her little sister crawling into her bed and snuggling close to her while she cried. Deborah remembered how Ava Jane had suffered.

Today, they were at Ava Jane's house finishing up a quilt she was making for Sarah Rose. The women had been working on the intricate appliquéd patterns all winter and now they needed to complete it before the spring chores, such as planting, gardening and canning, took over.

"Beautiful," Deborah said, her green eyes searching Ava Jane's face. "I think Sarah Rose will love this so much. The rose in the center is precious. It will make a wonderful present for her seventh birthday."

Ava Jane continued to stitch one of the black squares with white backings that would frame a colorful flower, bird or butterfly. "*Ja*, I'm thankful for the help. I have to work on it when the *kinder* are with Mamm and Daed." She glanced at the big-faced clock in the kitchen. Eleven in the morning. "We have a couple more hours. Daed is supervising the pony rides today."

Both of her children were learning about

chores and responsibility thanks to help from her parents. Daed provided a good male influence that helped to discipline them properly, but he couldn't be with them all the time.

Jacob. She always thought of what a good father he'd been.

"Gut," her sister said in a conspiring tone, bringing her back to the task at hand. "Now you can tell us what you think about Jeremiah Weaver coming back to Campton Creek."

Ava Jane missed a stitch and pricked her finger.

Which her shrewd and overly curious sister saw right away.

With a soft yelp, she dropped her needle and held her finger to her lips, the metallic taste of blood making her wince. But she didn't dare look at her sister or her suddenly quiet friends.

Deborah handed her an old remnant of fabric to hold over her finger. "You've talked to him?"

Ava Jane held the fabric to her skin, the pain of the tiny cut stinging through her with a warning while the pressure she put on the wound only reinforced her anxiety. "Not intentionally, *ne.*"

Why did she feel the need to defend herself and him?

"Then how?" Deborah asked, concern mixed

with hurt in her eyes that her sister had not confided in her.

Ava Jane glanced at the two other women watching her with a ridiculous intensity that made her want to laugh. But she couldn't laugh. "I was coming out of Hartford's and he was there on the street, loading some lumber into a truck."

"Lumber, on the street? And a truck at that?" her friend Hannah asked, her brown-eyed expression full of awe. "What does he look like now?"

Did her friends think Jeremiah had grown two heads and now breathed fire? Well, remembering how she'd recoiled at first, she'd probably acted the same.

Ava Jane swallowed and wished she hadn't been so transparent here today or with Jeremiah yesterday. She never could hide her emotions. Tenderhearted, her *mamm* called her.

Holding her head up, she said, "He looks healthy." *And hardened and world-weary.*

Jeremiah had always been formidable, but now his shoulders seemed to be even wider than she remembered. Strong shoulders.

Her sister made a groaning sound. "*Ja*, I suppose he would at that."

"I've heard things," Hannah said, speaking

in a rush. "Heard he looks like a different man now. *Englisch,* my *daed* says."

"Does everyone know he's back?" Ava Jane asked, unable to stop her own curiosity.

"*Ja,* and that he talked to you on the street," Hannah replied. "Grossmammi heard it from Rebecca Lantz. She said he's been taking baptism classes already."

Ava Jane shook her head. "No wonder it's all over the place." Rebecca Lantz loved to gossip and she'd also had a severe crush on Jeremiah at one time. Now at least, she was married and settled. But she still didn't know when to stay quiet. "Rebecca likes to prattle too much," she blurted.

She also told herself that if Jeremiah was attending baptism sessions, he must be back for good.

"We are not to judge," Leah, older and married with six children, said while she cast her gaze across the creamy quilt backing. "Ava Jane might rather not talk about this."

"He looked fine," Ava Jane said to show them she was unaffected and that she, for one, wouldn't judge. "We spoke briefly and I left."

She didn't go into detail about dropping her groceries or how Jeremiah had helped her salvage what she could. Nor did she tell them that seeing him had shattered *her* into a million pieces. She'd thought her grief was becoming better but now she mourned Jacob's death in a raw, fresh way. She blamed Jeremiah for that. He'd brought out too many emotions in her.

"Has he returned for *gut* then?" Leah asked, sympathy and understanding in her brown eyes.

"I didn't ask. And it's not my concern."

Hannah supplied the rest, her brown eyes settling on Ava Jane. "According to what I'm hearing, he's come home because Isaac is dying. Jeremiah will take over the farm chores and continue the carpentry work he and his father used to do together. His father needed him a long time ago. At least he's home now. Beth is happy. She never gave up on her brother."

This time, when her friend looked at Ava Jane, there was a trace of regret and condemnation in Hannah's expression.

What did she know about heartache? She had yet to find a husband.

Ava Jane went back to stitching her daughter's quilt, her face burning, her eyes misting. She was pretty sure she made a mistake in laying the pattern, but then some believed no quilt should be perfect anyway. Only God held perfection.

A good reason to remember she shouldn't judge.

The women went on to other topics such as

the upcoming Campton Creek Spring Festival to be held next month. The Amish had always participated in the fair. They took their wares into town and held a sidewalk sale in the park by the creek and across from Hartford's. But her sister's hand over hers brought her head up.

Deborah gave her a quick, quiet smile and then went back to stitching a yellow-and-white butterfly.

Her sister knew her so well, Ava Jane thought. Well enough to know Jeremiah being home *was* a concern. A big concern.

A few days later, Ava Jane's mother and sister came for an early-morning visit. *"Wilkum,"* she said, surprised to see both of them there on a fine Friday morning. "Come in."

Her family lived just around the curve, close enough that she could walk across the field and then take the covered bridge over the big creek between her land and theirs. She sometimes avoided going that way, though, and instead took the lane that wound away from the deep creek that held the same name as the town.

She visited with them weekly and her folks often stopped by to check on her. But usually that occurred when the children were just returning from school up the road. They loved their grandchildren.

This was an unusual visit.

"We need your help," Martha Troyer said, giving Ava Jane a quick hug. "We dropped by to see if you'd like to ride over to the Weaver place with us. Moselle is having a hard time of trying to take care of Isaac, and we've brought food to take." Then Mamm gave a little shrug, but her intent was soon clear. "I just felt that I needed to visit with Moselle this morning."

"And she felt that *we* both also needed to be there with her," Deborah said, giving Ava Jane an eyebrow lift that warned her this was not Deborah's idea. "Are you busy?"

Her dear sister was trying to give her an out.

Ava Jane searched to find an excuse. She'd already worked in the garden, swept the porch, hung some laundry on the line out back and made two chocolate pies. *"Ne,"* she finally said. "But why do I need to come along?"

Her mother gave her a soft smile. "I thought it might cheer up Beth. We haven't had a good housecleaning frolic in a long time, and Beth's been working by her *mamm's* side day and night for the last few weeks, helping to take care of Isaac. You two can distract her while I help Moselle with whatever needs doing. It'll be *gut* for Beth to talk to women close to her age."

Ava Jane couldn't say no. And besides, she wasn't sure Jeremiah's parents even knew he was back. But they'd have to know if he'd come back to help out. Everyone must have heard by now. He might be living here again, but he'd been using a truck in town when she'd seen him several days ago. That meant he might prefer life with the Englisch. But he must be living somewhere near here, at least. She wondered if he'd decided to stay out there in the world, after all.

But either way, surely he wouldn't be at his parents' place. He was no longer welcome there, from what Beth had said about their father's wrath.

Of course, Ava Jane hadn't been the best of friends with Beth through the years. Their friendship had been tested mightily. Maybe a visit could help that.

"Let me freshen up and get my bonnet," she said, already tugging at her work apron. "I made two chocolate pies. I can take one of those to go along with what you've provided."

Deborah gave her another meaningful glance and stepped back to mouth, "Sorry." Martha's all-knowing gaze moved between the two of them.

Did Mamm know what she was asking of Ava Jane?

Chapter Three

"I appreciate everything you've done for me," Jeremiah said, his hand over Mrs. Campton's, while they sat in the stately den of the big house he remembered so well.

Judy Campton smiled over at him and shook her head, her misty green eyes centered on Jeremiah. "No, son, we are the thankful ones. You made a great sacrifice, doing what you did after our Edward died. He would be so proud of you."

Jeremiah didn't feel proud. He'd done his duty and he'd followed orders, but he didn't know how he could ever wipe the stench of death and destruction off of his body.

"I did what I had to do at the time. I thought I'd make a difference, but so many died. So many. In spite of being wounded I managed to be whole and survive. I got to come home."

Judy nodded and patted his hand before she

sat back in her comfortable chair and took a sip of tea, her faithful housekeeper and assistant, Bettye, hovering nearby. Looking into Jeremiah's eyes before skimming her gaze over his blue cotton shirt and broadcloth pants held up by black suspenders, she said, "But you're not really home quite yet, are you?"

"No, ma'am," Jeremiah said, his coffee growing cold on the Queen Anne table centered between the two chairs. "I wanted to thank you and the Admiral for allowing me to stay in the guesthouse for this past couple of weeks. I needed to get my bearings and being here helped."

"I wish the Admiral felt like sitting here with us this morning," she replied. "He so loves talking to you. Makes him feel close to our Edward."

Admiral Campton had taken a turn for the worse over the last year. He had a private nurse and was resting in his bed now, but some days he managed to get up and sit out in the garden he'd always loved. It was a garden Jeremiah had helped landscape and plant all those years ago, he and Edward working side by side with the hired yardman.

"I'll go up and see him before I leave," he finally said. "I won't be that far away. You can get in touch with me if you need anything."

Mrs. Campton nodded, her pearl earrings shimmering along with her short white hair. "I know you'd come immediately, Jeremiah. But your family is depending on you. I think God's timing is always perfect, so you go on and get settled. But I expect you to visit whenever you're in town. Please."

Jeremiah saw the anguish on her face and heard it in that plea. They'd lost their only son and now they had no grandchildren to carry on the Campton name. When he'd called and asked to come by for a short visit, they had immediately taken him in and sheltered him, because they understood what he'd been through. He loved them like he loved his own family but he couldn't be a substitute for their son. And they couldn't fill the void inside his heart, kind as they were to him.

"I will always come and see you," he said, getting up to stand in front of the empty fireplace. Staring up at the portrait of Edward in his dress uniform hanging over the mantel, he said, "I only knew him for a year or so but he changed my life forever."

"Do you regret knowing him?" Judy asked, her tone without judgment.

"No," Jeremiah said, turning to smile at her. "He was one of the best friends I've ever had, and he did not pressure me in any way to join up. I regret that I didn't understand exactly what I'd be getting into. I don't mind having been a SEAL. But the torment of war will never leave me."

"You have PTSD, don't you? Post-traumatic stress disorder is a hard thing to shake and I suspect you, of all people, know that."

Judy Campton was a wise and shrewd woman who'd been a military spouse for close to forty years. She and Ed, as the Admiral liked to be called, married late in life and had Edward a few years later. Like his father, Edward had lived and breathed the military. And he'd given his life for that loyalty.

"Jeremiah?"

He looked around the big rambling room with the grand piano, the exquisite antique furnishings and the rare artifacts from all over the world. This place brought him both peace and despair. "I have nightmares, yes. Bad memories. Moments where I have flashbacks of the heat of battle. But I'm hoping that will improve now that I'm home."

"Or it could get worse," Judy replied. "I can give you the names of some good counselors."

Surprised, he shook his head. "I don't need that right now."

"I see." Mrs. Campton didn't look convinced. "There is no shame in getting help. I used to volunteer at the veteran's hospital about thirty miles from here. I've seen a lot of men and women improve by just talking about things."

"I'll be fine," Jeremiah said, "once I'm back where I belong."

"As you wish," Mrs. Campton replied. "But call me if you ever need me. I'll be right here."

With that, he made his way to her. When she tried to stand, he said, "Don't get up. I only wanted to tell you *denke*. I owe both of you so much."

She gripped his arm and pushed with a feeble determination, so he helped her up. "And as I said, *we* owe *you*. Having you home brings a little bit of Edward back to us. Now, you go to be with those waiting to see you again."

"I'll tell the Admiral goodbye before I leave."

He helped her back into her chair and alerted the nearby housekeeper that he was going upstairs. Then he turned and headed toward the curving staircase.

"Jeremiah," Judy Campton called, her gaze lifting to him. "Don't tell him goodbye. Tell him you'll be nearby."

Jeremiah nodded and took the stairs in a rush.

Once he left here, he'd head straight back to his parents' house and he'd be living there from now until…

Until he could make amends, prove himself

worthy and…maybe one day ask Ava Jane to marry him.

His sister, Beth, and his mother, Moselle, had welcomed him with open arms the other day since the bishop *had* told them of Jeremiah's wish to come home and help out. The bishop had talked this over with the ministers, too. They were all in agreement that as long as he followed the rules of the Ordnung and worked toward being baptized, he would be accepted back.

"Du bliebst Deitsch," the bishop had warned him. You must keep the ways of your people.

Mamm, perhaps too tired to turn down the help of her only son, had rushed into his arms the minute he'd walked into the familiar house two days ago. Then she'd stood back and said, "Go and see your *daed.*"

"He doesn't want to see me," Jeremiah replied, every pore of his body working up a cold sweat, his too-tight shirt straining at his shoulders.

His mother put her hands in Jeremiah's. "He needs to know his son made it home."

When he hesitated still, she added, "Do this for me."

Jeremiah couldn't deny his *mamm.* So he nodded and made his way into the hallway that lead to what used to be a sewing room in the back. His father lay there in a hospital bed, his body gaunt and pale, his once-thick dark hair now thin and streaked with gray. A shroud of sickness hovered over him, but with his eyes closed, he looked at peace and as if he was only napping.

Jeremiah blinked away the hot tears piercing like swords in his eyes. Had he caused this in his *daed*? Standing at the foot of the bed, he remained silent and asked God to give him the strength he needed.

I need forgiveness, Lord. I need my earthly father to know that I made it back to him. And You.

Now this morning, as he stood in the same spot and again prayed about how to approach his father, he could at least know that he'd never turned away from God. God had been there with him in the raging seas when he'd swum through treacherous waters and on the smoke-covered battlefields when he'd crawled with the snakes. God had been there when he'd held a buddy in his arms and watched the life leaving his eyes. God had been there when Jeremiah had woken up in a hospital and cried out for home. And for his God.

He had scars on his body and scars in his soul.

But how did he heal this rift that had separated him from this man? The man who'd loved him and taught him all the ways of being a real man. The man who'd cried out in anger that Jeremiah was never to enter this house again.

Talk to him.

Both the bishop and his mother had said the same thing.

So Jeremiah took a deep breath and used his military training to focus. And then he sat down in the hickory rocking chair beside the bed and let out a long shuddering sigh of both relief and regret.

"I'm home, Daed. I'm home for *gut*."

Isaac Weaver didn't respond. He kept right on sleeping in that deceptively peaceful way. But Jeremiah talked to him anyway, in gentle, hushed tones that held both respect and sadness.

He began to tell his story of taking a bus across the country and finding a job in Coronado, California, where the US Naval Special Warfare Command was located. He'd lived in a hut of an apartment with two other roommates who were planning to join up, and he had worked at restaurants and on farms while studying to get his GED. He'd saved up some money and passed the test, thanks to the books Edward had encouraged him to read and to his well-educated and worldly roommates who to this day still called him Amish. He'd then joined the Navy and immediately asked to enter the SEAL Challenge Program. He'd entered the Delayed Entry Program as an enlistee, so he could be sure he knew what he was doing and get some extra training and instructions before the real stuff began.

The instructors and counselors had warned him that training and duty would wipe out everything about him and change him. And still, he had insisted he was ready.

"No one can ever be ready for such a thing," he whispered in anguish. "But I couldn't fail. I would have had to go back to fleet—regular Navy for two years—that is." He stopped, shuddered a breath. "I didn't fail. In spite of everything, I made it through."

His father never moved, seemed to barely be breathing.

Jeremiah sat quiet for a while, his prayers centered on his father and this farm. He made a list in his head of all he needed to do. And he was just about to go on to explain boot camp and how the grueling training he'd undergone in a facility in Illinois, known as The Quarterdeck, had just about done him in. So close to his home and yet he couldn't reach out or visit.

He never got that far, however.

Because he heard feminine laughter in the

front of the house…and smelled lavender and fresh soap.

Standing, he peeked up the narrow hallway to the front of the house and saw three women hugging his mother and sister.

And one of those women was Ava Jane Graber.

Ava Jane glanced up and into the other room.

Jeremiah stood staring at her, his expression full of surprise and hope. He looked so different today. He was wearing the standard uniform of an Amish man: work shirt, broadcloth pants and dark work boots. He pushed the straw hat back, as if he'd become irritated with wearing it again.

Ava Jane couldn't move, couldn't breathe. This had been a very bad idea. She should have stayed at home, where she belonged.

Jeremiah started toward her and then halted, his boots creaking against the hardwood floors.

Her mother and sister stopped talking and stared at her, and then they both glanced to the end of the hallway.

Deborah's curious stare held shock. "So, Jeremiah is back."

Beth nodded, her glance dancing over Ava Jane before settling on the others. "*Ja*, indeed he is. Home to help out."

"I'm glad to hear that," Mamm said, patting Mrs. Weaver's hand. "And to see that he's visiting with his *daed*." She sent Ava Jane an apologetic smile tempered with a motherly warning.

"Isaac rarely responds to anyone these days," Moselle Weaver said. "We hoped Jeremiah might bring him back."

Ah, that explained why Jeremiah was in his *daed's* room. But Ava Jane wondered what would happen if Isaac Weaver should wake and find his wayward son sitting there.

Dear Lord, help me to be kind. Help me to find grace.

Jeremiah was now coming toward her, determination gathering like a thunderstorm in his eyes. He made it a few feet into the room and stood firm, his expression almost serene. "Hello, Mrs. Troyer. Deborah." His eyes moved from them to her. "Ava Jane."

Mamm hurriedly greeted him and turned back to Beth and Mrs. Weaver.

But both Beth and Deborah stood mystified by this encounter, knowing expressions passing between them like *kinder* playing volleyball.

"We only came to drop off this food and offer our help," Mamm said, holding up the baking dish full of chicken potpie. "I believe Ava Jane has a chocolate pie for you, too."

Ava Jane's hands were shaking so much she thought she'd drop the pie.

But before that could happen, two strong

hands took the dish right out of her grip. "My favorite," Jeremiah said, his smile soft, his tone quiet. *"Denke."*

The rest of the women started scurrying here and there like squirrels after acorns. Nervous chatter filled the big room and echoed off the crossbeams, but Ava Jane couldn't hear what the women were talking about. She only heard the roar of her pulse pumping against her temples.

So she stood there like a ninny, wondering what to say or do. Ava Jane needed the floor to open up and swallow her. Needed the wind to lift her up and out into the wide-open spring sky. Neither of those things happened.

"How are you?" Jeremiah asked, true concern in his eyes.

"Fine, thank you," she managed to say. "And how are you?"

A loaded question. *What are you doing here? How did this happen? Explain everything to me and help me to understand.*

His smile reminded her of the old Jeremiah. Her Jeremiah.

"I'm *gut*. Better than when I first arrived."

"So...you're going to stay here with your family now?"

"Ja. I was staying with the Camptons in their guesthouse."

The Camptons.

Like a cold splash of water, sharp-edged anger hit her in the face. "That makes perfect sense," she said, regaining her equilibrium and her strength. "Why didn't you continue to stay with them?"

Jeremiah's expression shifted and went dark. "Because they are not my family. I belong here. And I'm going to prove that to everyone, Ava Jane. Especially to you."

Shocked at his blunt words, she ignored the rush of embarrassment surging through her and accepted that he held bitterness in his heart, too. *Gut.* She hoped he had a lot of guilt and bitterness left to deal with.

Regretting her harsh wishes, she nodded and swallowed her pride. "Your *mamm* needs you now. But you don't need to prove anything to me, Jeremiah. Nothing at all."

Praying they could leave now, she turned to face her mother. But before Ava Jane could form a good excuse, her mother announced, "We've been invited to stay for dinner. I've accepted only because after we eat, we are going to give Moselle and Beth a rest while we clean the house and wash up the laundry."

Her mother's tone brooked no argument. Ava Jane took a long breath and reminded herself that she had come here for Beth and Mrs. Weaver. Not for him. She could share a meal with these two friends. She'd be just fine because she would not let Jeremiah's presence affect her. At all.

But before she could hurry into the kitchen, Jeremiah moved closer. "I have everything to prove to you. But mostly, I have everything that is left in me to give to God."

With that, he spoke briefly to his mother, then nodded to the other women and turned to walk out the back door.

Ava Jane's face burned with shame.

She'd never once stopped to wonder about what he'd been through out there. And she had to consider—did he truly have anything left to give to God? Or her?

Chapter Four

The women ate a quick dinner, and then Ava Jane, her mother and Deborah did a thorough cleaning of the Weaver house while Moselle and Beth tended to and then sat with Isaac. After an hour or so of sweeping, dusting and freshening up, the smell of lemon-scented furniture polish and bleach gave the whole place a clean spring-time freshness. They'd thrown open all of the windows, and a gentle breeze cooled the entire house and cleared away some of the gloom of medicine and sickness.

The whole time Ava Jane's nerves were on edge. She kept expecting Jeremiah to come through the door and glare at her again. She didn't belong here but she was having a hard time seeing *him* here. He didn't belong and he stood out like a mighty oak in a field of corn.

Father, help me to overcome this resentment.

I know he means well but he left us. He left all of us.

Her prayers didn't calm her, and yet Ava Jane tried to wipe the bitterness out of her mind and go about the task of helping friends in need. Since Jeremiah had left, she'd stayed away from the Weaver house. But she'd been friends with Beth since they were close in age and had attended school together, even if Ava Jane had let things lapse in that friendship. Civil. She'd been civil to his family and she'd been sympathetic to their pain. *Ja*, she felt that same pain to the core.

Maybe that was why her mother had forced her to face the entire family head-on. So she'd see her own bitterness and work to overcome it. Her parents had a way of embracing adversity instead of turning from it. Her mother was forcing her to face her worst fears and work through them with prayer and guidance.

Indeed, she had to put her raw feelings aside. Isaac was dying. And his only son had come home to help out and be with him. Maybe she should talk to the bishop and get some advice on how to handle things better.

"I can't thank you enough," Moselle said over and over after Mamm had told her they were done. Coming out of the sick room, she'd gasped in surprise at the fresh flowers on the table and the sparkling clean kitchen and sitting area, her eyes as blue as her son's. Patting her *kapp*, she added, "I've neglected so much around here."

"Mamm and I try," Beth explained with an embarrassed blush. "We hurry through chores because we want to sit with Daadi as often as we can."

"Of course you want to spend time with him," Mamm said with a sympathetic smile. "That's why we came to help."

"We're blessed to have *gut* neighbors who do the outside chores," Moselle said, grief in every word. "I'm thankful Isaac is home with us and we can be near him."

Not to mention cleaning him and bathing him, Ava Jane surmised from hearing their conversations. No wonder the two of them looked so withered and exhausted. And no wonder they'd welcomed Jeremiah back with open arms. He was needed and she had to admire his stepping up to do the right thing.

That took courage, considering how he'd been gone for so long. Considering how he'd left and what he had become.

Father, can I ever forgive him? How can I even start?

Beth had voluntarily filled them in on the details earlier, her voice hushed and whispery. Ava

Jane hadn't wanted to hear it but she'd held her breath with each revelation Beth brought out.

"He is staying in the *grossdaadi haus* for now. The bishop approved that. He takes his meals with Mamm and me, but doesn't sit with us." She shrugged. "His choice, out of respect for Daed."

He was here to work hard and help his family, she explained. In the meantime, he planned to make things right with the church. With God.

"He started the baptism sessions weeks ago."

Deborah glanced at Ava Jane during these tidbits of information regarding Jeremiah. "Where has he been for so long?" Deborah asked, her innocent tone barely masking her inquisitive nature.

"Out in California," Beth said. "At least that's the address he sent me a year ago, after he'd finished his duty. But I didn't tell anyone except Mamm." She shrugged. "He joined the Navy and went on some sort of secretive missions. I don't ask for details. I think whatever he did out there must have changed him. He needed to come home."

She shot Ava Jane a beseeching, hopeful smile.

Ava Jane didn't tell Jeremiah's sister or mother that she'd searched in the library to learn about the Navy and the SEALs. Why bring that up now? She hadn't asked any questions while Beth talked either, but now she tried not to think about Jeremiah being out in the world alone. She only knew he'd have to make a lot right in order to be brought back into the fold. That was the Amish way. The bishop and ministers had obviously approved of him coming back. He'd have to study and understand adult baptism, discipline, shunning and separation to see where he fit in and to accept that once he committed and was baptized, he'd be expected to stay here and follow the church rules.

Once Jeremiah confessed his sins in front of the church and asked forgiveness and was baptized, he would be accepted. They would not mention his past again. And he would become Amish again. For good.

Could he do that? Could he confess what he'd done all these years, just forget all about it? How did a man forget about killing and war? What if he wanted to go back out there into the world or go back into the fray? What about that *duty* Beth had mentioned?

If he left again after he'd pledged to serve God and return to the tenets of the Ordnung, which consisted of a district-wide set of rules and regulations they were all expected to observe, Jeremiah could never return.

Please, Father, I pray he means to stay.

She refused to feel anything beyond that hope, but her heart hurt for what he must have done in the name of war. He had courage, too much courage. He'd always had a reckless, rebellious side and he defended his friends, no matter what.

Honoring a friend was why he'd left in the first place.

But he was back and he was indeed trying to make amends. Ava Jane knew she wasn't to judge. That didn't mean she could forget either.

She could only pray for Jeremiah and hope for the best for him.

The shining thankfulness in Moselle Weaver's eyes told Ava Jane one thing. He was still very much loved. And love could heal a multitude of sins.

"I think that's it," her mother announced from behind where Ava Jane stood by the sink, staring out toward the fields.

They'd finished in time for Ava Jane to make it home to greet her children after school. "*Gut.* I need to get back before the *kinder* put out a search party."

She was about to turn to leave when she saw Jeremiah plowing, his broad shoulders firm and solid, his big hands working the reins with a seasoned knowledge, as he urged the two big Belgian draft horses through the hard dirt.

Growing up, he'd been muscular and big boned, his upper body full of strength because he managed to sneak off and swim in the creek all summer long. He'd had a natural grace about him. He'd been the kind of man who could take on any task and make it look easy. A smart learner, her *daed* used to say. Now that muscle was solid and fully matured and that grace fell across his broad shoulders like a mantle. He would farm this land and make it good again.

She didn't want to accept how natural he did look, back in the fields, his hair long and curling around his hat, his face bare to mark him as unmarried. When she thought of that and of all the unmarried friends she had, a streak of fierce jealousy shot through her like a spark of fire.

She would not be jealous. She had no right to be jealous of anyone who might be interested in Jeremiah.

Behind him in the far distance, the covered bridge stood solid and firm, a glisten of water peeking through in diamond-like sparkles. Beyond that, far on the other side of the big creek that ran deep and wide, stood Campton House. The huge Georgian-style mansion had always fascinated Ava Jane. But the house held bad memories for her, too. Jeremiah spent a lot of his *rumspringa* at that house.

Something fluttered inside her heart. A memory of Jeremiah and Jacob laughing and playing in the body of water centered in their community. Jeremiah loved to swim since the day his *daed* had begun teaching him. He'd glide through the water like a fish. Jacob hadn't been quite as strong but he tried to keep up. She'd watch them from the covered bridge, her fear of water too pronounced to allow her to join them. Jeremiah coaxed her to join even though girls didn't swim with boys.

"I'll teach you how to swim, Ava Jane," he'd said.

She'd never learned. And she'd never told him that she was terrified of the water.

Why had she remembered that now, when the man she watched was deep in rich dirt and misty dust?

"He's going to plant our spring garden even though it's late in the season," Beth said from behind, causing Ava Jane to come out of her stupor. "He's trying so hard, Ava Jane."

"I can see that," she said to Beth, meaning it. "I'm glad for him. You need him home, *ja*?"

"Ja," Beth replied. "God brought him home. Our prayers have been answered."

Thinking of the Biblical story of the prodigal and how his father had welcomed him with open arms, Ava Jane touched Beth's hand but didn't speak. Then she turned to her mother and sister. "I need to go now please."

She almost ran out of the room, her heart betraying her every step. She had to stay away from Jeremiah Weaver. He'd broken her heart once…and she was still mourning the loss of her husband. But she was still mourning the loss of Jeremiah, too. It was wrong to think of another man when she ached for Jacob every day.

Jacob had drowned down in the creek, trying to save a hurt calf. He'd slipped on some rocks and old limbs, fallen and hit his head. A neighbor had heard the little calf crying out and had found Jacob.

The prodigal might be home but her husband was gone forever. That didn't seem fair to Ava Jane. Not at all.

She would try her best to forgive Jeremiah for leaving her but she couldn't forget how badly he'd hurt her. The guilt of loving him haunted her. Even now.

Jeremiah stayed away from the house long after he was sure Ava Jane and her mother and sister were gone. He couldn't be around her right now. It hurt too much to see the disappointment in her eyes, to read the judgment in her expression.

Coming back here had been hard. He'd been

prepared for the curious stares and the condemning whispers. He'd also been prepared to work hard toward forgiveness and baptism. But he'd blocked out everything else. Or he'd tried. He thought he could get on with things if he avoided Ava Jane. Campton Creek was a small community and the Amish community within the tiny hamlet was even smaller. People knew he was back and, while most had been kind if not standoffish, everyone was watching him as if he were a deadly bug.

Shunned but not really shunned.

Alone in the middle of the world he'd loved and left.

Longing for a woman he'd loved and left.

Dear Father, I don't think I can do this.

"Jeremiah?"

He whirled, hoping.

But it wasn't Ava Jane walking toward him with a tall glass of lemonade. His sister, Beth, came up to the fence he'd been working on. "I reckoned you'd be thirsty."

"Ja." He took a long swig of the cool tart liquid. *"Denke."* His little sister gave him the curious expression he remembered so well. "Is there something else you need to say, Beth?"

Beth watched as the big Belgian geldings munched on their evening hay. "You stayed out here all day. You must be exhausted."

"I'm used to hard work." He glanced back toward the house.

"They have left, Jeremiah. You can come inside now."

"I'm used to being outside, too," he replied. "It's nice to be back on the land."

Again, that curious stare. "What was it like, Jeremiah? Out there, I mean."

His gut clenched. He didn't talk about such things. None of them ever did. For one thing, his team members were trained to stay quiet about their missions. But then, how could he explain it to innocent, pure Beth? Or anyone for that matter. The brutality of being in such a secretive, demanding career changed some men in ways that could never be explained. But he had refused to let it change him.

He did not want to talk about it either.

Instead, he did a scan of the landscape, his gaze hitting the big creek where he'd frolicked and played with Jacob, with Ava Jane sometimes watching from the shore or the bridge. "What happened to Jacob?" he asked.

Beth shot him a disappointed frown. "Did you not hear? I thought I told you in one of my letters."

"No. I didn't even know she… Ava Jane… was a widow. You never mentioned *that* in your letters."

"I did try to contact you, but later I tried not to mention *her* in my letters," Beth replied, guilt coloring her pretty eyes. "I didn't want you to think of a married woman, and then I only wrote about our family, since I didn't want to gossip or hurt you."

"I thought of her every day," he admitted. "Now, tell me what happened to Jacob."

Beth swallowed and held on to the weathered fence post. "He drowned down in the creek."

Jeremiah flinched and closed his eyes. "How? He was a fair swimmer."

"He went in after a trapped calf and, from what the sheriff could put together, he must have fallen and hit his head. They found a deep gash over his left temple. He was knocked out and went underwater. Just a foot or so of water."

Jeremiah hit a hand against the fence, causing the old wood to crack. Beth stepped back, shock in her eyes.

"I'm sorry," he said in a gravelly whisper, his heart rate accelerating. "I... I had to learn to swim one thousand yards in twenty minutes and to hold my breath for at least two minutes underwater. I mastered scuba diving, underwater demolition and swimming for miles at a time. I could have... I could have saved him."

Beth's expression filled with shock at what he'd blurted out, but she shook her head, a hand on his arm. "You weren't here, Jeremiah. And even if you had been, the fall caused him to go underwater. No amount of training or ability can change that."

"I should have been here," Jeremiah said, the rage at what he'd done bubbling up inside of him. "I should have been here."

He tried to move away but Beth held him still. "If you had been here, you would have been married to Ava Jane, and Jacob would have been somewhere else that day."

"Ja," he said, nodding in a rapid-fire gesture of anger. "Exactly."

Then he did pull away, leaving his confused, frightened sister to stare after him.

If he'd been here, everything would have been different.

But now that he was back, so many things had changed forever.

Chapter Five

A week later, Jeremiah stood in the hardware aisle at Hartford's General Store when Ava Jane came in, carrying a basket of muffins. Everyone praised her muffins and pastries, and he noticed Mr. Hartford kept a supply in stock at the store, which meant she was earning money by selling them there. Jeremiah had bought a couple. Good, sturdy muffins full of oatmeal, nuts and fruits. Carrot muffins, banana muffins, pumpkin, too. He even got ahold of a zucchini one and he didn't even like zucchini.

No fancy cupcakes for Ava Jane. She believed in hearty, stick-to-the-ribs food.

He watched now as she smiled shyly while Mr. Hartford bragged about her cooking skills to a couple of giggly female tourists out for a day of "experiencing all things Amish."

Ava Jane listened and smiled and answered

their questions with grace and patience. After the women bought a bagful of the baked goods right out of her basket, Mr. Hartford took the rest and placed them near the register.

Then Ava Jane turned to shop, her eyes meeting Jeremiah's, her serene smile fading into a wisp of air.

He caught up with her in the produce aisle, where tender seedling plants lined the bins near the fresh produce. "Hi."

"Hello, Jeremiah," she said, her dainty hand patting her bonnet. "How are you?"

"Gut," he said. "Just gathering some supplies to fix things around the place."

Sympathy colored her eyes a sad blue. "It must be hard, seeing your *daed* like this. He was such a fine, strong man. I'm so sorry."

Jeremiah had to swallow the lump in his throat. "He hasn't woken once since I've been home. I talk to him but..."

"He hears you," she said, something shifting in her attitude, her eyes softening, almost as if a wall had crashed down around her. "He hears you. It's *gut* you came home."

"Is it?" he asked, wishing it so. Wishing he could have come home to friendly greetings and a welcoming community. Everyone tolerated him, but Jeremiah wasn't sure he'd ever belong here again. The bishop and the ministers and the deacons were all probably shaking their heads about what to do with him.

He had to stay on course, stay on the straight and narrow. Surprisingly, his military training was coming in handy. He could focus. He could go into a zone and see things through to the finish. Because he wanted *this* now as much as he'd wanted *that* then.

He prayed every night. He prayed while he sat with his father. He prayed when he looked into Ava Jane's eyes.

Ava Jane looked shocked at his question. "It can be good, *ja*. Isn't that why you came back? To make things right again?"

He nodded and wished he could snap his fingers and fix everything. But the bishop had warned him this would be a long, hard journey. "I have a lot of work to do yet," he said. "I guess I'd better get going."

"Not all of your work will be out in the fields, Jeremiah," she said. Could she see into his heart?

He nodded, understanding. He had a lot to work through and most of it revolved around his feelings for her.

He was almost to the door when Mr. Hartford called out to him. "Jeremiah, you've been doing a lot of carpentry work since you returned. Ava Jane was just asking me yesterday about someone to help repair her back porch. What did you say, Ava Jane? A couple of rotten boards?"

Ava Jane turned pale, panic frozen on her face. Mr. Hartford had no idea about her relationship with Jeremiah. "It's nothing, really. I can find someone else. I shouldn't have even brought it up."

"I don't mind," Jeremiah said, sending Mr. Hartford a nod. "I'll come by later this week to see what needs to be done," he said to Ava Jane. "If that's all right with you."

She lowered her head and fidgeted with her apron. "That is fine. Mamm has been complaining about it and Daed keeps forgetting to fix it. Besides, I try to do things on my own and not run to my parents for every little thing."

Jeremiah's heart hurt for her. A woman alone with two growing children, trying to keep things together. She probably got up early to get her baking done.

"You don't have to run to anyone," he said. "I'll be by to look at your porch first thing next week."

He turned to leave before she could tell him no.

Sunday morning dawned bright and sunny with a slight crispness in the wind. But springtime freshness filled that same wind with various scents rising up: herbs and baked bread, bacon frying, the earthy scents of hay and animals and trees blossoming.

Ava Jane stood at her favorite spot in front of the kitchen sink, where the view of the valley and the water beyond always took her breath away. The sun peeked out over the rolling hills and winked through the newly budding trees. She remembered so many mornings waking up to this. Jacob would come up behind her and tug her close, his chin against her hair.

The water reminded her of two men. Jacob and Jeremiah. In a way, she'd lost them both to water.

Dear Father, how do I remember one when I'm trying to forget the other?

Ava Jane finished washing the breakfast dishes and called to the *kinder,* *"Kumm."*

Sarah Rose came rushing down the stairs, chattering like a magpie. "Eli won't hurry, Mamm. He's got one boot on and one in his hand. His hair needs combing—"

"Stop spluttering so," Ava Jane said with a smile. "Eli, what's taking so long?"

Her son seemed to move at a slow pace at times. He was a good boy but he did tend to get into trouble a lot.

She added one more prayer to her morning list. She needed strength to raise her children.

Strength and wisdom and purpose. She needed to teach her *kinder* obedience first and foremost.

Her parents were so good with the children, but Ava Jane knew she had to be tough on them in order to teach them the right paths in life. Eli was a constant challenge and Sarah Rose had a strong-willed personality.

Ava Jane might have softened since Jacob's death but she was gaining strength every day. Hadn't she managed to be kind to Jeremiah the other day at the general store?

And she'd be kind to him if he showed up to fix her porch. But that would be an uncomfortable situation.

At least it would save her having to pester her *daadi* about it. He had a bad back and she wouldn't have to add to that.

"Eli!" she called, frustration edging her tone.

Her son ambled down the stairs, his dark hair flying out in shiny clusters around his head. "I forgot my hat," he said, turning to head back up the stairs.

Sarah Rose shook her head and put her little arms across her midsection in frustration. "I don't like being late."

"Nor do I," Ava Jane confirmed. "Eli, you have sixty seconds. Sarah Rose will count."

She knew Sarah Rose could only make it to

fifty, but Eli came rushing down the stairs, his black felt hat crooked. "Here, Mamm."

"I'm not finished counting," Sarah Rose whined, her eyes going big and misty.

"You can finish counting on the walk over to the Miller place," Ava Jane said. "Now, let's gather our things and get on the road. It's a nice Sunday morning."

The Millers held services in their big barn. Jacob and most of the other men of the district had helped them build it a few years ago. The women had gathered and made food for the event. Barn buildings were always an event to see.

Now the tall, sturdy building had weathered a bit but it would stand the test of time. Not like her old farmhouse. Jacob had tried to keep up with the many repairs around the twenty-acre farm, but he'd never been able to get the place the way he wanted. He loved working the land and they'd made a passable income selling produce and grain, but in spite of her family's best efforts, she'd been forced to let some of the field go fallow. Now she sold baked goods, eggs and canned goods to make a living and tended a small garden so she could sell fresh produce and fruit at the local farmers market. She also made quilts, doilies, pot holders and aprons to help bring in extra income.

It wasn't a bad life, but it was a tiring life. Constant worry nagged at her. She had two children to feed and clothe and, while her parents helped, she could never catch up.

Ava Jane waved to a family passing in a buggy but her thoughts went back to the day she'd seen Jeremiah in the general store. Why she'd agreed to let him come to fix her porch was beyond her. She couldn't stop him now. She'd seen the determination in his deep blue eyes. There was something commanding about him that frightened her and made her wonder what he'd seen and done out there.

Steel. His gaze held a sliver of steel.

That had to have come from being trained to…fight and kill.

She couldn't think beyond that. She couldn't imagine what he'd been forced to endure in the name of justice and democracy. And yet, beyond that steel, she'd also seen a brokenness, a crack in the armor he'd had to put on.

That armor would have to be pulled away, piece by piece, if he wanted to become Amish again.

When she looked up to find the crowd gathering at the open barn, she saw Jeremiah standing alone, away from the friendly chatter and greetings and hugs. Her heart stalled to the point that she stumbled and almost dropped the apple pie she'd made yesterday.

"Mamm?" Both of her children stared up at her in surprise.

"I'm fine. Just hit a rough patch."

That was the truth. She'd been limping along, coming to terms with her grief, that never-ending grief that tore at her soul and woke her up at night in a cold sweat. But she'd begun to see some light in all the darkness of her grief.

Until now. Now she stumbled forward, caught in the grip of despair all over again. Jeremiah not only reminded her of how much she missed Jacob, but Jeremiah brought back all the pain and grief she'd suffered through when he'd left her in the middle of the night.

Twelve years gone and now back here in the flesh. Back with so much between them, so many changes in his appearance and in his heart.

But she'd changed, too. Or had she, after all?

How would she come to terms with the not knowing, with the still wanting? With the guilt and fear and thoughts of him rushing over her like a spring flood?

"Are you all right, Mamm?" Sarah Rose asked, true concern in her eyes.

"Of course I am," she said, smiling down at her daughter. "Just clumsy is all."

Ava Jane lifted her spine and declared that she would make it through somehow. She always had. Obedience first. Obedience to God and the tenets of her faith.

She told herself that she had to keep moving. So she carefully made her way toward the sanctuary of the barn. With each footstep she took toward the man standing there, looking as lost as a puppy in the middle of the road, Ava Jane's fear diminished, to be replaced with a determination to obey God and show compassion for someone who was once lost but had now been found.

She owed Jeremiah that much, didn't she?

Jeremiah could feel the stares being shot like arrows toward his back. His sense of his surroundings had been hewn to the point that he knew when someone was watching him or approaching him. Even now, he stood with his back against the wall so no one could sneak up on him. Not that they could, but he didn't want to whirl in defense and send young children screaming in the other direction.

So he stood silent and still as Eli Graber approached him with a serious expression on his face.

"Hey," Eli said, his eyes piercing Jeremiah

with so many memories. The boy looked a lot like Jacob.

"Hey, yourself," Jeremiah replied, nodding. "How are you this fine morning?"

"Gut," the boy replied. "My friends told me you know how to shoot guns."

Jeremiah lifted away from the wall. "I do. Why are you asking me about that?"

"Just curious," Eli replied. "My *daed* had a squirrel rifle, 'cause they were messing in the corn bin."

Jeremiah squatted so he could be at eye level with the boy. "You do know to never touch a weapon without an adult supervising, don't you?"

Eli bobbed his head. "Yes, sir. Mamm won't allow that either. Only when Grossdaadi is around."

"What's this all about?"

Jeremiah stood to find Ava Jane glaring at him, anger tinging her pretty eyes.

"The boy is curious. He's heard talk about me."

Ava Jane's eyes went wide. "Eli, go find your sister."

Eli took off like a missile launching, leaving Jeremiah to face the protective fury he saw in Ava Jane's eyes. "I didn't encourage him. He mentioned a squirrel rifle."

"I hid it away from him," she replied, fear mixing with her anger. "Why would he ask you about that?"

Jeremiah had to be honest with her. "He asked me if I know how to use a gun and I told him yes, since his friends had already informed him of certain things regarding me. But I also told him he should never touch a weapon without an adult nearby."

He expected her to reprimand him but, instead, Ava Jane shook her head and let out a sigh. Glancing around, she said, "People will talk, Jeremiah. I'll speak to Eli and explain to him he is not to listen to gossip. No matter that it has a thread of truth in it."

With that, she turned and marched away, her head and her bonnet high, still in a tiff.

Progress, he thought with grim amusement. It was a start.

And now he had to face the rest of them. Inside during the service. Another step he had to take after already getting curious stares from the young adults in baptism classes with him.

He'd always considered himself courageous, but now he was quaking in his boots. Maybe he should wait awhile before attending church.

Then Jeremiah felt a hand on his shoulder. Ava Jane's *daed*, Samuel Troyer, stood there with a slight smile and what looked like expectation in his wise hazel eyes. Mr. Troyer was a minister. He'd had to approve Jeremiah's return.

"*Kumm*, Jeremiah. You don't want to miss the first sermon."

"No, sir," Jeremiah said, his head down. This would be the beginning of his redemption.

But he wouldn't have true redemption until Ava Jane forgave him.

Chapter Six

Dawn crested over the pasture, the sun's early rays as muted and soft as the gentle cooing of the mourning doves strolling underneath the old live oak.

Jeremiah sat down in the chair beside his father's sick bed and took a deep breath. His father's once-virile, strong body had sunk into itself. Isaac's jawline lay slack and withered, and his once-thick, dark hair had now turned thin and streaked with gray. Labored breaths lifted and lowered his frail chest enough that Jeremiah could see the outline of his ribs underneath the nightshirt he wore.

"*Gut* morning, Daed," he said, his voice low but sure. He grew stronger each day while he had to watch his father grow weaker. "I tended the livestock. We have two fine new baby lambs, two growing pigs, and our milk cows are hearty. We are up to ten now. Mamm and Beth have chickens now. And ducks, too. The fields are tended, too. The garden is planted with tomatoes, corn, lettuce, beans and peas, and your favorite, brussels sprouts. The seedlings are that beautiful fresh green that signals spring. We're a bit behind but we'll catch up. I'll make sure of that."

Isaac continued to sleep, his breath the only sign that he was still on this earth.

His *daed* hated brussels sprouts.

Jeremiah swallowed and held his hands together. He'd been back at home a couple of weeks now and the quiet, steady routine had helped him keep things in perspective. He cherished these times with his father. "I attended services yesterday. Sang the old hymns, listened to the sermons and the Scriptures. Prayed. Had another lesson on being baptized. I'm going to do it, Daed. I'll be the oldest to be baptized this year, but my *rumspringa* is finally over." He chuckled. "The young kids look at me with a mixture of curiosity and aversion. They don't know what to make of a grown man sitting there with them."

He wished his father would respond. Open his eyes and touch Jeremiah's hand. But the doctors didn't hold out much hope that Isaac would ever wake again.

So Jeremiah lowered his head and prayed. He thought about the tenets of his faith: obedience, humility, following the Ordnung. He'd listened, and after the service, he'd been more at peace but still at odds. Where did he belong? He hadn't been able to sit and eat dinner with his sister since the men and women ate separately. His mother had stayed home with his *daed* so he hadn't been able to look to her for encouragement.

He almost left after the service, but this time Ava Jane blocked his path.

"You must be hungry," she said, a bit of mirth in her words. "The ministers went on a bit today."

Jeremiah's back ached from sitting on the hard bench. "*Ja*, but I felt the emotions in the words. Even the High German ones that I don't really understand." Staring over at where the long tables were filling with people, he said, "I've truly missed all of this."

She smiled at that. "You need to stay and eat. There's a spot beside my *daed*."

Jeremiah followed the direction of her pointing finger. "I sat by him during the service. He might be tired of babysitting me."

"He's not babysitting a grown man, Jeremiah," she replied, true kindness in her eyes. "He's encouraging and standing with someone he cares about. He approved your return and he will stand by that. Go and have some food."

"Someone he cares about," Jeremiah said now, after telling Isaac the whole story. "Samuel Troyer is a *gut* man. He could have turned away from me, because of who I was before. But he didn't. I'm thankful for that kindness."

And he had a kind daughter. But would she always be so kind? Or had she felt obligated to show him compassion since they'd just attended church?

He wondered about her changing moods toward him, but he also understood the battle she fought against.

Jeremiah kept that notion to himself.

He'd see her today. This morning. He'd be near Ava Jane while he repaired her porch. He could enjoy that, at least.

For now, just being near her would have to suffice.

He had to get his head on straight and stay focused on the task ahead. He knew the bishop and the ministers were watching him. He couldn't mess this up. So he treated this new training in the same way he'd treated training to become a Navy SEAL: with the dignity and respect it merited. Failure was not an option. In both cases, one slipup meant you were out for good.

Jeremiah took in a deep breath and then went back to talking to his father.

"I think I told you about how I made it into basic training. But getting to that point was hard. First, I had to find work and study to get my GED. I had a little money tucked away, and I answered an ad for a roommate and wound up sharing an apartment with two other boys. They helped me get a job washing dishes at a nearby restaurant and, I think I told you, they helped me to get my high school equivalent degree. I passed on the first try, mainly because of all the books Edward had told me I needed to read, but those two helped me a lot, too. *Gut* men who also planned to join up. During my downtime, I swam in the apartment building's pool and out in the Pacific Ocean. It never gets too cold in California, but I swam even when it was chilly. I wanted to pass all the necessary tests."

Hadn't he already explained all of this to his father?

He stopped, remembering how he'd been probed and checked and questioned over and over. They'd done a background check on him and he'd had to do some tall talking to show the Navy that he was serious. He'd been so afraid they'd turn him away. But one personal reference had cleared him. Edward Campton's parents had vouched for him. That and he'd worked hard to make sure he had everything in order, even taking courses in mechanics and shop and talking with counselors and instructors about the reality of his decision.

"I worked hard, Daed, and made it through the first draft," he whispered. "I showed my Dive Motivators that I was committed. But that is nothing compared to coming home and facing the people of Campton Creek. Nothing compared to sitting here with you. I love you so. I want you to know that. I came back for you and our family and our faith. I will make this right."

He lifted his head and watched his father for signs of acceptance. Signs of life.

Just that ragged, harsh breathing, that sinking in and out of his father's once powerful body.

Jeremiah stood. He wanted to touch his father and hold him close but…he didn't feel quite that worthy yet.

Wiping his eyes, he turned and put on his hat. He would get through this. He'd made it through yesterday's whispers and stares. Ava Jane and her family had made sure he would.

Jeremiah didn't understand why her family had been so kind to him when he'd broken her heart and gone against his faith. They could have chosen to shun him, but the Troyers had always been looked up to in the community. Her *daed* was a minister. Maybe he had to set an example. Maybe that was all. If the Troyers set the standard, the rest of the community should follow suit. Their compassion touched him and burned him to the core. Did he truly deserve it?

Jeremiah would accept that bit of kindness and compassion. In the meantime, he'd show all of them that he was worthy. He'd fix her porch and make that right. One step at a time.

God had a way of showing the signs of life to those who were out on the road. Especially to those on the road toward home.

Ava Jane kept checking the road. Jeremiah said he'd be by today and she was as wired as one of the barn cats trying to chase a broom. Her children were in school and she was alone.

Always alone.

The acceptance that she'd worked so hard to create, that illusion that she could do this on her own, she wore now like a frayed quilt. Jeremiah's coming home had magnified her loneliness and made her bitter and antsy.

"I don't want to be bitter and antsy," she said to the wind. "I want to be gracious and secure in my faith."

When she heard a buggy jingling up the drive, all thoughts of remaining calm lifted out the window on the billowing lace curtains.

Jeremiah was here.

She watched as he stopped the buggy and secured the petite carriage mare near a grassy area by the barn. Then he gathered his tools and stood for a minute, his gaze moving over the barn and fields.

What did he see out there? Her father had helped her plant a small vegetable garden and she had chickens and two milk cows. She canned food and made quilts and baked breads to make a living, and her parents helped out with offerings of meals and labor. But her little farm always looked forlorn in her eyes.

Did he see it the same way?

Ava Jane swallowed her trepidations and went out on the porch, her *kapp* fresh and her apron clean. Not that she'd gussied up for Jeremiah. No. She just liked to start a new day with crisp possibilities.

"*Gut* morning," he called from the barn, his smile tentative. Tentative and shattered as if he, too, were afraid to be here.

Was he as nervous as she felt? Were his big, sturdy hands trembling and his heart pumping too fast?

"*Gut* morning to you," she managed, gaining strength with each deep breath. "A fine April day, isn't it?"

"*Ja,*" he replied. "Easter is coming."

"Easter." A few weeks away now. A new

beginning, a fresh start. Maybe she should consider what Easter could mean for her and Jeremiah. Maybe she could be kind to him, just kind.

Kindness cost nothing, after all. Civility could hide all the hurt in the world. She could be cordial and civil.

But her heart bumped a longing that went deeper than kindness. Ignoring that longing, she nodded toward the rotten porch floor. "Daed's back has been bothering him something awful, so I've managed to hide this with rugs and such, until Eli slid on the rug and sent it flying. Then my parents saw the damage. I told them not to fret, but Daed keeps promising he'll fix it. And then he gets busy and forgets."

"He'll see it fixed next time he comes," Jeremiah said, his gaze awash in so many emotions that it reminded her of a storm cloud. "I've brought lumber and tools, so I'll get started."

"Yes, of course," she replied. "I'm sure you have lots of work back home, so you'll want to get this done and over."

He nodded while he sorted his tools. "Always. But the planting is done and the milk cows are healthy. I've cleaned out the barn and made repairs there. I have ideas for some improvements, too. One day."

"Modern improvements?" she said, wondering if he'd try to add in technology and the things of the world since he'd been out there and experienced such things.

"Maybe a tractor," he replied. "But I haven't decided yet."

"A tractor?" She didn't mean to sound so judgmental. She knew some Amish used tractors around their barns to help run things.

"Don't worry. I won't force you to go joyriding with me. The tractor would stay off-road."

She almost laughed but caught herself. Giving him a huffy glance, she whirled. "I can't stand here sputtering all morning. I've got chores. It's laundry day."

She could feel his gaze on her departing back. "So instead of sputtering about you'll be wringing out?"

"Something like that, *ja*," she retorted. At least he couldn't see her smile. But in spite of frowning on the tractor idea, smiling at his jokes felt good. Too good.

An hour later, Ava Jane ventured toward the sawing and hammering noises to check on Jeremiah's progress. He'd gone about his work with quiet intention, not bothering her one bit.

Well, he was bothering her but he didn't know that.

She'd tried to get the wash done and hung on

the line that wasn't far from where he'd bus-ied himself with tearing out old porch planks and replacing them with new ones. Ignoring Jeremiah had proved to be harder than she'd imagined. She'd gone out the front door and around the house so she wouldn't have to step near where he worked. But he'd noticed that and shot her a questioning stare to show she wasn't fooling him.

Not an easy morning.

Now each time she glanced toward him with shy precision, Jeremiah worked on as if he didn't have a care in the world. His focus on his task was impressive. He walked to the buggy and picked out a couple of boards, measured, sawed, pondered, his brow furrowing into ruts as deep as the plowed ones in the field.

What was the man thinking anyway?

He was thinking how natural she looked there, hanging clothes on the line. The sunshine hit the sheets and towels and allowed the fresh-scented, clean items to send a sweet perfume his way. The perfume of home and family and happiness and a kind of normalcy he'd missed these many years.

He watched with a covert control honed by years of stealth and wished he could go to her and take her into his arms and spin her around.

The ache of knowing that would be wrong nagged him like a wound that wouldn't heal.

He had so many of those kinds of wounds. But being here, his lungs filling with the clean, clear essence of Ava Jane, his senses remembering the peace of this valley and this place, helped to soothe the parts of him that were still broken and aching.

So he worked and pretended not to notice the woman who worked beside him, yet away from him. He worked and he watched and he calculated and he measured and he wondered and he prayed.

This morning, right now, this was what faith and hope were all about. In his world, the only easy day was yesterday.

Today was for hard work, the work that required doing even better than yesterday.

At least, with this work here right now, he was near her.

Just near her.

Jeremiah was so lost in his thankfulness he didn't even realize she'd gone back inside. But when the back door opened again and he looked up and into her eyes, he smiled.

"I have lemonade and a blueberry muffin... or two."

"Two should do it," he said with a grin. "I

think once I've eaten those, I'll be up to finishing this porch."

After placing a tray with two large glasses full of the icy liquid and a plate with two muffins on a small wooden table between two rocking chairs, she said, "*Kumm* and rest a bit, Jeremiah."

Such simple words but to Jeremiah they sounded like a request from heaven.

Nodding, he placed his saw on the porch railing. "*Ja*, I think I will at that."

This was the kind of rest that could save a man's soul.

Chapter Seven

A week later, Ava Jane sat in the rocking chair on the back porch, waiting for Sarah Rose and Eli to come home from school. Admiring the fresh planks and new coat of paint underneath her feet, she held Callie, her favorite calico cat, and allowed her mind to wander back to having Jeremiah here. After they'd sat and shared the muffins and lemonade, small talk about life in general keeping them on safe topics, he'd gone right back to work and she'd gone about her chores inside.

"You don't have to repaint the whole porch," she had said later when coming out to wait for the children to return from school. Noticing he'd found a broom and swept the porch clean and that a can of whitewash and a brush sat at the ready, she had to argue a bit. The new boards did stick out in a very noticeable way but she hadn't expected him to paint, too.

Jeremiah shrugged off her protests. "No bother. Won't take long. I had the paint left from some touch-ups I did for Mamm. The old place needed some spring freshening, too. And I thank you and your family for helping with that. So this is my way to return the favor."

Deciding not to nag him about the extra work, Ava Jane nodded instead. "You mean the day we came and cleaned for your *mamm*? That's what friends are for, Jeremiah." Hesitating, she added, "Although they had to twist my arm a bit to get me to come along."

He finished sweeping the porch and put the broom away. "Because you didn't want to see me?"

"I was afraid to see you," she admitted, steeling herself for his reaction.

"I think I can understand that. I was shocked to find you standing inside the house." He reached for the broom again and held it like a sword, his eyes dark with regret. "And now?"

She took a breath, so many emotions converging inside her head like a river stream flowing straight to her heart. "Now I've accepted that you're back."

"But you still don't want me here, right?"

"It's not up to me to want you here or not,"

she replied, the tone of that declaration softer than she'd planned. "You are here now and you have good reasons for returning."

"But you don't think I should be here at all."

"So you can tell that just from being around me?"

"I can see it in your eyes."

Deciding they needed to let this subject go, Ava Jane stood to stare down at where he propped a brogan-covered foot on the bottom step. "No matter how I feel, my duty is to accept you and not judge you."

He stared at her with eyes that held so many secrets but with a connection that could not be denied. "I want you to forgive me, Ava Jane."

How should she respond to that gentle plea? "I'm trying, Jeremiah. I pray for you on a daily basis."

"*Gut*, because I'm not going anywhere, ever again," he responded, propping the broom against the porch railing. Then he gave her another soulful stare. "Are you afraid of me, Ava Jane?"

"Should I be?" she countered, thinking by the way her heart was pumping, she ought to be afraid. Truth be told, he scared her in more ways than one.

"No," he replied. "You don't ever have to be afraid of me. Whatever I became out there," he said, waving his hand in the air, "I left behind out there."

"Are you sure about that?"

He stopped and stared off into the distance, giving her an answer loud and clear. "I can never be sure of anything except that God brought me home and I'm sure in my faith. My faith never wavered, but I did."

He sure did. He wavered enough to leave her sobbing in the night to go off on some dark duty that only he could understand and she needed to remember that. But she didn't tell Jeremiah her thoughts.

Instead, she said, "I'm not afraid but I don't want you feeling that it's necessary to make amends to me."

"Isn't that what friends are for," he echoed, "to help others and make amends when needed?"

"Okay, we'll stop on that note," she replied, more frightened of the conversation than she was of him. "We can agree that we have to make the best of things, so I'm making it a point to accept you back into this community."

But it ended there.

He nodded as if he knew exactly what she was thinking. "I'm going to paint the porch on either side and leave the middle open. If it's okay with you, I thought I'd ask Eli if he'd like to help with that part."

"He'd be happy to dabble in paint, I'm sure," she said, thinking Eli needed a strong male to influence him. Only she still wasn't so sure that person should be Jeremiah. Eli was already far too fascinated with him, so she'd warned the boy not to pester Jeremiah. She hoped Jeremiah wouldn't pester her boy either. "But you've been here all day. Shouldn't you go?"

Jeremiah stood up straight and looked into her eyes again in a way she both remembered and now found different—stronger, hard-edged and way too determined, his expression cut in stone. "Do you want me to go?"

Yes. No. She didn't want to delve into the strange feelings he provoked in her. "I'm not trying to get rid of you. I just don't want you to neglect your own family in order to help mine."

"You, you mean," he said. "You don't want me to help *you*."

He was messing with her head. "I didn't say that either."

"Then what are you trying to say?"

Lifting her hand out of frustration, Ava Jane said, "Fine. Stay as long as you want. Stay past dark if you need to. But don't expect supper."

He laughed and kept right on at his work.

And now here she sat a week later, rocking away, her thoughts as jumbled and tangled as new barbed wire. Jeremiah had finished the painting, along with Eli, well before supper. She could still hear the echo of their masculine banter, Eli asking rapid-fire questions and Jeremiah patiently answering with care and consideration. Not a word about weapons or war had come up, thanks to his easy way of steering the conversation back to the chore they were finishing together. He'd left with a wave and a smile.

Which had been a shame. She'd made fried chicken and had planned to set an extra plate.

Jeremiah sat by his father's bed, wondering if he had the energy to stay awake much longer. The work didn't bother him so much. He was used to hard work and discipline. But being back in a community where every move he made was scrutinized and measured caused him a lot of anxiety and discomfort. He remembered feeling that way growing up and it had got worse once he became friends with Edward Campton.

Why had he been so tempted by the world out there?

Maybe I deserve to be judged and criticized.

Now, however, he wanted to be here. Right here. He'd told Ava Jane he'd left all of that behind him. He wouldn't make the mistake of running away again. He'd have to take whatever came his way and deal with it based on the rule of surrendering his will to God. In the Navy, he'd had to surrender himself to his instructors and superiors to be broken down and made new again—stronger, more dedicated, more demanding and completely compliant. It was the same here, only this time his will was being softened and measured and renewed with hope and love instead of death and despair.

He honestly didn't know which was harder. This soft breaking could tear him apart much more than being a warrior ever had. If he lost her again…

"I can do this, Father," he said to the Lord. "I will do this for You." He'd put God first and hope the rest would fall into place, the Lord willing.

He often read to his *daed* from the Scriptures at times such as this, when the doubt and shame covered him like a tattered blanket, revealing all of his flaws.

"I carried this Bible with me, Daed." Jeremiah rubbed his hand over the worn leather volume that Mrs. Campton had insisted he take when he'd gone to tell the Admiral and her goodbye.

"You'll need God's word now more than ever, Jeremiah," she told him in her calm cultured voice. "Edward always had his Bible with him and now we want you to accept this as our gift to you."

They'd had it engraved with his name. "Because the Lord named you before you were even born," she reminded him.

"Do you think the Lord had this in mind for me then?" he asked, wanting to know he'd made the right choice.

She smiled up at him. "I think we have to take many paths before we find the way home. God knows your heart. No matter what, as long as you keep your faith, no matter how many right or wrong turns you take, you will find the right path. And you will come back home again."

She hadn't needed to add that sometimes that meant in a body bag or inside a flag-draped coffin.

Jeremiah had never been without this Bible. It was worn, scarred, battered, the pages dog-eared and stained from battle and from his fingers moving over them and turning them.

He opened the book at random and landed on Psalms. And so he read to his unconscious father. When Beth and Mamm came in and quietly took their seats, Jeremiah kept on reading, his mind on the words of the beautiful lamenting prayers, his head cast down as he remembered the whispers and stares each time he came upon a group of Amish men. Some, such as Ava Jane's father and the bishop, had been kind to him. Others not so much.

He thought about Ava Jane and the wonderful day he'd spent at her home last week. Since then, he'd tried to avoid her because it just hurt too much. He'd thought being near her would cure him. But this malady couldn't be cured by nearness. He wanted all of her. Her forgiveness, her love, and her in his arms.

That would help take away the sting of judgment and curiosity that others cast upon him. But he couldn't expect that. Not now. He still had to earn the Father's love and forgiveness and he still had to earn his dying *daadi's* love and forgiveness.

He finished the chapter and looked at his father and then he looked over at his mother and sister. "I'm sorry, Mamm," he said. "So sorry."

His mother pushed out of her chair and came to his side, her hand on his arm. Jeremiah stood and she took him into her arms and held him. "You know I've already forgiven you, son."

"I want Daed to know, to hear my pleas just as David wanted the Lord to hear him."

"Your *daadi* hears you," she said, her hand touching Jeremiah's hair. "He knows just as the Lord knows."

Beth stood by their mother, tears in her eyes. "Jeremiah, would it help if we listen to you and let you tell us what you've been through?"

Jeremiah pulled away and shook his head.

"No. I'm not ready for that. You're not ready for that. I... I need to check the livestock."

With that, he turned and hurried from the room, that feeling of being unable to breathe overtaking him. He could hear the choppers overhead, could hear the screams of women and children and the rapid fire of machine guns, could see the startled faces of the enemy being taken down. Those sights and sounds moved through his dreams with an echo of sorrow and urgency. Two of his team members had gone down. He'd had to get to them. He'd tried to save them.

He'd failed.

No, he wasn't ready to share the horror of what he'd seen with his precious sister and mother.

Maybe not even with his father.

Only the Lord above knew that story and knew his heart.

When he reached the barn, the misty night air hitting his feverish skin, Jeremiah stopped and held tight to one of the big, heavy doors.

Maybe he should start this healing journey by trying to figure out how to forgive himself? How could he expect true forgiveness from others if he didn't have the courage to look himself in the eye and offer forgiveness to the man he'd become?

Leaning against the solid door, Jeremiah looked toward the heavens. He'd often lain on his rucksack in the middle of the desolate mountains and looked up at the stars. On those nights, he'd wondered about Ava Jane and missed her with each rush of pulse that moved through his temples.

He missed her still, under this sky, the same sky but different now. A peaceful night sky with only the sound of animals settling in and the wind whistling like a hymn against his skin. He was safe here. His pulse slowed, his mind calmed.

A horse whinnied nearby, bringing him out of his musings.

Jeremiah looked up at the crescent moon. "I have to make it all right before I can even think of a future with Ava Jane. She's still not sure of me. I'm still not sure of myself."

And he wanted to be sure, very sure, this time. Because once he had her back, he would not leave her side again.

So he did the deep breathing he'd learned to keep calm in battle and he focused on what was coming next.

The spring festival was coming up. His mother and sister were excited about displaying the quilts they'd worked on all winter and possibly selling a couple, but they weren't sure they both could attend. Ava Jane had mentioned she would be selling her baked goods—muffins and pies and cakes and bread—to make extra money, along with some other wares she and her sister and fiends had been working on. Her friends would set up booths at the festival, too. Raesha Bawell and her mother-in-law would be selling hats they designed and made by hand for both the Amish and the Englisch. They'd all need help with moving and setting up in the big town square.

Jeremiah would volunteer where he could and do whatever needed to be done. The spring festival always brought large crowds of locals and tourists, too. He could blend in and still be a part of things without feeling as if he were on display for everyone to ponder and whisper about.

Deciding he'd talk to Mr. Hartford, this year's festival chairperson, first thing in the morning, he went about checking the animals and thanked God for presenting him with enough tasks to keep him busy and tired.

The more he worked, the less time he'd have to dwell on what might have been and what could still come to be.

Today. He'd take each day at a time and concentrate on today only. Because every SEAL knew the only easy day was yesterday. And Jeremiah was pretty sure the good Lord knew that, too.

Chapter Eight

Ava Jane had lots to keep her occupied and she was very glad for that. These past few days had whizzed by with a busy-bee buzz, giving her plenty to keep her mind off of Jeremiah.

She and her friends had finally finished the rose-patterned quilt for Sarah Rose. She planned to give it to her on her upcoming birthday, which was about a month away. Sarah Rose would have a small party here in the backyard, complete with cake, cookies, lemonade and tea. Her friends would bring small gifts but Ava Jane couldn't wait to give her daughter the child-sized quilt, made especially for her little bed. She hoped Sarah Rose would cherish it in the same way she cherished quilts from her mother.

Today, however, Ava Jane focused on the many treats she hoped to sell at the spring festival this weekend. She'd made dozens of cookies, including every kind from chocolate chip to snickerdoodles to peanut butter. She'd made breads and rolls and pies, enough so that her gas-powered refrigerator was becoming completely full. Today, she planned to take a batch of her creations into town to store in Mr. Hartford's big refrigerator since the festival was only a couple of days away.

The back screen door opened with a squeak. "Hello, I'm here to help."

"In the kitchen, Deborah," Ava Jane called to her sister. Deborah loved to help her bake and they often talked about opening a café together, but her nineteen-year-old sister insisted she wasn't ready to get married and settle down.

Ava Jane figured that would change in a couple of years. Deborah already had her eye on Matthew Miller. Just like Ava Jane and Jeremiah, Deborah and Matthew had grown up together and were about to go through *rumspringa* together.

Ava Jane said a quick prayer for a better outcome for her sister. She'd lost Jeremiah during his *rumspringa* but…she'd found Jacob. They'd soothed each other after he'd abandoned them and one thing had led to another. They married a year and a half after Jeremiah left. Now even though she'd lost him, she had two beautiful children, thank the Lord.

I waited for you, Jeremiah. She had waited, at first hoping and praying that he'd change his mind and come home. Then she'd waited because she hadn't known what else to do.

Her family had sustained her, telling her she'd be okay, telling her that Jeremiah had to find his own way. They'd been as surprised and shocked as she when she'd finally managed to explain. Deborah had been so young, only eight years old at the time. But Ava Jane remembered her little sister crawling into her lap and hugging her tight.

When things between Jacob and her had changed from friendship to more, Ava Jane hadn't waited any longer.

Was I meant to be with Jacob all along? she wondered silently while her sister prattled on about the weather and the garden and—

"—four horns and two goatees," Deborah finished rather loudly.

"What?" Ava Jane squinted and blinked. "What are you talking about?"

Deborah put down the bag of baking supplies she'd brought and grinned over at Ava Jane. "I've been talking about this goat I saw down the road, but you weren't listening so I added a few details."

"Four horns?" Ava Jane asked, rolling her eyes. "Are you sure about that?"

"No, just checking to see if you heard a word I said." Deborah adjusted her work apron and moved around the wide, clean kitchen, her green eyes as bright as the corn popping up in the field beyond the yard. "Are you okay? You look tired."

Ava Jane lifted her hand in the air. "Of course I'm tired. I've been baking double time for a week now and putting the finishing touches on Sarah Rose's quilt and trying to keep things going. I've got gardening and flower beds and weeds and the chickens—they lay a lot of eggs. You know how busy planting season can be."

"Don't I," Deborah said, finding the coffeepot right away. "Mamm's pulling out her hair with her own crafts for our booth and tending the gardens. Daed seems to be slowing down a bit." She stopped and shook her head. "He's been so forgetful lately."

Ava Jane had noticed her father's slower gait lately and agreed. It wasn't just his physical appearance. His mind drifted a lot, too. "He's getting older but he doesn't want to admit that."

"His back is really bothering him," Deborah said. "Mamm stays on him to see about it but he doesn't like going to the doctor."

"No man does," Ava Jane said, remembering how Jacob would fight her tooth and nail whenever he had an ache, even a cold.

How she missed him. When her thoughts turned from Jacob back to Jeremiah she blinked and tried not to think about the time she and Jeremiah had spent together last week. *Forced* time. She'd only sat and talked with him to be kind, but now she wished she hadn't encouraged so much as a friendship between them. But… she had to wonder if he had scars that were hidden and if he refused to get help for those scars.

"There you go again," Deborah said, poking at Ava Jane. *"Was der schinner is letz?"*

At her sister's concerned expression, Ava Jane shook her head. "Nothing is wrong, I promise. Now, can we get to work?"

"It's Jeremiah, isn't it?" Deborah said with a note of persistence. "I heard he was here last week."

Ava Jane tried to frame her response in a neutral tone. *"Ja*, he fixed that bad spot on the back porch."

"And painted it, according to my sources," Deborah said on a smug note.

"And just who are your sources, sister?"

Deborah shook her index finger in the air. "You don't need to know that, but your *kinder* have eyes in their heads, in case you haven't noticed." Then her green eyes went dark and soft. "I worry about you. He broke your heart. Why is he hanging around?"

"I hired him to fix the porch so Daadi wouldn't have to do it," Ava Jane said on a determined but defensive note, thinking she'd be wise to heed Deborah's observation regarding what her children saw, heard and repeated. "Our parents have been kind to him and I'm trying to follow their example."

Deborah snorted. "Right. Daed has a duty to be kind to a prodigal. You don't." Leaning over the big table, she stared at Ava Jane. "Is there something more between you two?"

"Nothing else, sister," Ava Jane said, meaning it. "You know how much I loved Jacob. But I can't turn away from Jeremiah."

"So you're trying to honor both of them by letting Jeremiah work on this farm?"

Ava Jane set down the milk she'd pulled from the refrigerator. "He was Jacob's best friend. He's trying to prove his worth and make amends. And besides, Mr. Hartford suggested him and it was hard to turn him down right there in the general store." Shrugging, she added, "He wouldn't let me pay him in cash. Instead, he only asked for a pound cake for his family. Said it was his *daed's* favorite. But we both knew Ike wouldn't be able to eat the cake. I made it anyway."

"And had someone else deliver it?"

"Yes, but then you probably already knew that."

"So how do you really feel about him?" Deborah asked, her hand on Ava Jane's arm.

Ava Jane gave up and blinked back tears. "Honestly, I don't know. One day I'm okay with him being back and the next I wish he'd go away. It's been so hard. I don't know what to do."

Deborah took Ava Jane into her arms and held her close. "We pray. I'm sorry. I shouldn't have forced this issue but I know you so well."

"Too well," Ava Jane said through her tears. "But I'll be all right. God brought him home. He will have to answer to a higher calling. I'm not to judge but I can't forgive him solely based on his offer to repair some things for me."

"*Ja*, and he'll have to make greater amends—and repairs—than just touching up a porch," Deborah replied, stepping back to let go of Ava Jane. "But I'll go by your example and pray for him. I just don't want him to hurt you again."

Ava Jane nodded and quickly wiped her tears. "You were so young when he left that I'm surprised you'd remember anything about Jeremiah. Why are you so fierce about this?"

"I was young," Deborah said, her gaze on Ava Jane, "but I remember hearing you cry at night. And you know me. I listened when you poured your heart out to Mamm. It's hard to forget that kind of anguish even if I didn't quite understand it at the time. But all these years I've heard the story of what happened between you two. Makes me not want to fall in love."

Ava Jane had never stopped to think about the ripple effect of her misery or about what others might have been spreading all this time. "I don't want you to think that way. I was happy with Jacob and I have the *kinder*. I'm happy now. You'll find someone one day and you won't have to pour your heart out to anyone."

"Except my sister," Deborah said, smiling over at her.

"Always," Ava Jane replied. "Now, enough of this pity party. We have work to do."

Her sister went off to fetch more bowls and baking dishes.

Ava Jane stood there with her heart raw and frazzled and wondered how she'd ever get through this.

Trust in the Lord.

She clung to that remembrance and prayed the prayer from Proverbs 3:5 that taught her to lean not on her own understanding. And with each blueberry muffin she made, she tried not to dwell on how much Jeremiah had enjoyed eating blueberry muffins with her last week.

He now made it a point to look for the blueberry muffins each time he entered Hartford's General Store. That day last week with Ava

Jane had sustained Jeremiah over the past hectic days.

His father was getting worse. The home health-care nurse told them it wouldn't be much longer. Jeremiah sat with him as often as possible, until late into the night and sometimes in the early dawn. He'd told his father things he'd never tell another living human being. But then his father probably didn't even hear him.

With some of the savings he'd set aside while he was in the military, Jeremiah hired a day nurse to help his mother and Beth. They both looked haggard and exhausted and neither was able to turn his father or change the bedding. The male nurse was strong and a good worker. He and Jeremiah could get the work done in record time. With the added home health care, his mother could get some rest and his sister could go back to being young and visiting more with her friends.

"Thank you, son," his mother had said, tears in her eyes. "Your father wants to die at home. I couldn't bring myself to put him in a nursing facility far away."

"Nor do you need to be going back and forth," Jeremiah had replied. "Don't worry, Mamm. I'm glad some good can come from the money I saved up."

"You might need it one day for yourself,"

Moselle had said, her gaze full of hope. "If you marry."

"We'll worry about that time when it comes," he'd told her with a quick hug and a peck on the cheek.

"I'll pray for that until the time comes," she'd responded.

In the meantime, he had the crops and livestock to tend, cows to milk and a dozen other things to keep him occupied. Helping set up for the festival had been a blessing, too. Mr. Hartford had recommended him for handiwork and so he had side jobs that should last through the summer. By then he should be done with his reintroduction to the church and he'd be ready to be baptized. Ready to start his life here all over again.

But until then, he had Ava Jane's rare smiles to spread warmth throughout his heart. While he prayed to the Lord to give him redemption, he also asked the Lord to bring him peace. In case Ava Jane couldn't forgive him. He would live the rest of his life right here with her nearby. He had to be able to accept that and let her go before he could bring himself completely back. But what if Ava Jane found someone else?

Either way, he had a tough row to hoe.

Now, after grabbing a muffin and a cup of coffee, he went back out onto the main street of Campton Creek and admired the hard work he and several other men had put forth.

Campton Creek was a beautiful little town anyway, but with newly blooming flowers he couldn't name cascading in bright reds, pinks, yellows and purples from huge sturdy clay pots that lined the quaint streets, it looked like the perfect picture of America.

The America he'd fought for, the home and town and people he'd defended. Why had he felt such a strong need to turn away from this simple, peaceful life and go into an unknown, dangerous world that had left him scarred and shattered?

Maybe because he wanted to preserve this and keep it just as beautiful as it looked this morning.

Standing here now in the midday sunshine, Jeremiah wondered how he'd ever made it home. Other dark thoughts pushed at his consciousness but he refused to let them in. He was here now and that had to count for something, didn't it?

He headed to help set up a big tent in the park by the creek when he heard a ruckus down the street. Turning, he spotted a group of Amish trying to get around several young men and women who looked like tourists—or maybe bored locals—with cameras and cell phones flashing while they laughed and made jokes. Jeremiah watched for a moment and then turned back in the other direction. Best to keep on walking when those kind were around.

Until he heard one of the Amish women cry out, "Stop that."

Jeremiah whirled back around and his chest tightened. Ava Jane and her sister, Deborah, along with two other women, were now cornered by two men from the group.

One of the men touched Deborah's bonnet and said something that made the others laugh. Deborah tried to go around but one of the girls stopped and blocked her path. "Why do you wear that funny thing anyway?"

Ava Jane grabbed her sister with one hand, her basket full of baked goods in the other, and tried to hurry away. One of the men moved toward them again and pulled at the ties of Deborah's *kapp*.

As the women tried to step around, the man turned to his buddies. "Did you get that on the video?"

When he turned back to laugh at the women, he ran smack into Ava Jane and knocked her basket to the ground.

Jeremiah didn't think. With a red rage coloring his vision, he ran up the street and grabbed the brawny man and shoved him up against a wall, his arm pressed against the man's throat with enough pressure to cut off his breath. "You will respect these women, understand?"

The other Englisch parted and scattered, while the shocked man in his grip stared at him with a fear he'd seen over and over again in the enemy's eyes.

"Hey, we were just having some fun," the man said with a weak plea. "Let me go, man."

Jeremiah tightened his grip and flipped the man around to face the others. "Apologize."

But before the man could form a word, a gentle hand on Jeremiah's arm broke through the burning haze in his brain.

"Jeremiah, let him go please."

Ava Jane.

He backed away, still glowering at the red-faced, sweating man who now rubbed a shaky hand down his throat.

"I'm sorry," the man said, his nervous gaze moving over the four Amish women. Then he took off before Jeremiah made another move.

Jeremiah stared after the group that continued up the street and then turned to Ava Jane. If he'd thought he'd seen fear in the man's eyes, he was mistaken.

The fear and terror he saw in her eyes was real and alive and as shattered as his heart. He'd scared Ava Jane and her sister and friends. And he'd scared himself.

"I'm sorry, too," he managed to say through deep breaths, a cold sweat chilling his entire body. He tried to reach for her then dropped his hand. "Are you all right?"

She didn't speak. Shock colored her eyes and her skin had turned pale. She looked at him as if she didn't know who he was, fear and embarrassment clear in her misty eyes.

Jeremiah glanced at the other women but they, too, stood still and quiet, afraid to make a move. His head roared with that familiar dread, the kind he had when he awoke from the nightmare of reliving a battle. What did they see in him now?

Someone much more dangerous than a misguided Englisch man who didn't show respect?

Deborah stepped forward, her eyes wide and wary. "Thank you, Jeremiah. We're both okay."

Ava Jane whirled and dropped to her knees, trying to gather her damaged items, her hands shaking. The others followed suit, trying to salvage all of her hard work. Jeremiah wished the earth would swallow him. Everywhere he looked, people had stopped to stare. At him. At what he'd just done.

He bent down beside her and reached for a crushed loaf of what looked like nut bread.

"Stop it," she said in a heavy whisper. "Please, Jeremiah, don't help me again in that way. In any way."

Here they were, right back on the street, exactly in the same way as when she'd discovered he'd returned. She had that same shock and disgust in her eyes again.

They'd come so far and now he'd made a mess of things all over again.

He sank back, his hands on his knees, his gaze on her. But he saw it there, the shock, the rage, the confusion and the disapproval. She'd seen the worst of him right here today. He'd been fully prepared to rip that man's head off simply because he'd touched Ava Jane.

Jeremiah stood, every fiber of his being shaking and recoiling from what he'd become, while dark, horrible memories cackled through his head with a clarity that outstripped his nightmares. Sending her one last pleading glance, he turned and stalked away from the prying eyes of others and the crushing hurt in her ragged gaze.

His body coiled and tightened, his head pounded with each step, the rush of flashbacks almost overtaking him. But he didn't stop walking until he looked up and saw Campton House looming like a beacon over him.

And because he didn't have any other safe haven right now, he stalked up the steps and knocked on the door.

Chapter Nine

"Did you have a flashback?"

The quiet question didn't match the deep concern he could see in Judy Campton's still-sharp eyes.

Jeremiah took another drink of the water Bettye had brought him after Mrs. Campton had ushered him into the living room. He stared at the crystal goblet full of crushed ice and with a slice of lemon and strawberry. Mrs. Campton always believed in making her guests feel special.

"Jeremiah?"

Glancing up, he shook his head, his heart rate decreasing now, the cold sweat chilling him in the drafty old house. "No, ma'am. But I could feel that rage of battle overtaking me. I had to blink...and get a grip on things." Or he would have gone too far.

Thinking of Ava Jane's gentle hand on his

arm, he finally faced the woman sitting across from him. "Ava Jane was there."

Looking confused, Judy put a pink-polished nail to her cheek, her diamond solitaire glistening in the soft light. "Oh, the girl you were to marry all those years ago. I see her sometimes in town. She's a marvelous cook. Bettye brings home her cakes and muffins all the time."

Standing, he took his water goblet with him to stare out at the bulging colors and fluffy blossoms of the formal garden in the sprawling backyard. "Yes, she makes extra income from her baking." He explained how he'd seen them with the young Englisch kids. "One of the young men insulted her sister and then almost knocked Ava Jane down. She dropped her basket of baked goods."

Judy tapped her fingernails against the brocade of her chair, her shrewd gaze moving over Jeremiah's face.

"So you wanted to defend her honor, of course." She waited a beat and then added, "Because you still love her."

"Yes." He turned back to her again, the relief of that confession lifting his shoulders and allowing him to breathe again. "But she saw my rage in my actions and she does not tolerate that. Ava Jane always was a gentle soul so it's hard for her to imagine me being a SEAL. I'm not sure she even knows what that means, but she knows enough to realize I have fought against others and…killed men in the line of duty. And she certainly remembers that I chose that over staying here to make a life with her."

He explained how Ava Jane had married his best friend and now was a widow with two children. "She resents me but things were getting better between us. We shared some pleasant time last week when I went to her house to repair some bad spots on the back porch. Now, after today, she doesn't want me around." Holding his straw hat in his hand, he added, "Today, she saw the real me."

Judy stared up at him with understanding. "She doesn't know what you've been through and she doesn't understand your reasons for doing what you did. Have you tried talking to her about it? About what your duties entailed?"

"No, ma'am. I don't want to frighten her even more and it's hard to talk about what I saw. What I had to do. Things I'm not ever supposed to repeat."

"Edward wouldn't talk much about what he'd done either. It's the SEAL code, of course, for reasons of national security and for protection of themselves and their families—never talk about the mission." She leaned forward. "However, I know Edward shared more with you than he ever did anyone else. Maybe because he trusted your dedication to your faith."

Jeremiah heard the irony in that statement. "A faith I left."

"Did he push you to join up?" she asked, the question rushing out in a way that made Jeremiah wonder how long she'd wanted to ask that question.

"No, he never revealed anything specific when he talked to me. He always stressed how tough it was to become a SEAL. So much so that I knew it all by heart. He gave me books to read and showed me the history of the Navy, but he was brutally honest about the hardness of it all. He never once suggested anything to me about joining. Edward thought he was safe with me and so he told me things he could never tell anyone else. And yet, the day he died I knew I had to go and fight in his honor. But I can't explain that to Ava Jane. I don't even understand it myself. And that might keep us apart forever."

Judy Campton shifted, her blue skirt crinkling. "But that rule of not talking makes it hard on everyone. We need to open our sorrows and our memories and be purged, so we can heal, so we can forgive, so others can forgive us."

Jeremiah sat down again. "Who do you talk to?"

"God," she said with a serene smile. "Ed

would talk to me but only about his love for his work. But then, he never went through what you and Edward did. I think sometimes he wishes he had, so he'd have that bond with Edward. He so wanted our son to become a naval officer, but he respected Edward's choice to join the SEALs."

Jeremiah stared up at the portraits and medals lining the wall, wondering again about how much this precious woman held tightly inside her heart. "Your husband is a hero in his own right."

"Yes, but he's tired now and he wants to be with our son." She lowered her gaze, and Jeremiah saw a slight crack in her control. "Let's get back to you."

"I shouldn't have bothered you," he said, glancing at the clock. "I need to go back to work."

"You are never a bother," she said, waving him back down when he tried to stand. "Ed is sleeping but you are welcome to go up and say hello."

"I… I need to finish helping with the tents for the festival," he said, another kind of panic crashing around him. "I sit with my father almost every day and I don't think I have the strength to watch both of them die. I'm not ready to face that with the Admiral, too."

"You have more strength than you realize,"

Judy replied, her teacup rattling in her shaking hands. "We both do. Ed is ready to go. We've had a good full life, with both happiness and heartache. But that's what life is all about. It's also about second chances. You have the strength to stay the course, Jeremiah. Or you wouldn't have come back here."

Jeremiah hurried to help her set her empty cup back on the side table. "I thought I did. Thought I could do this. But today I realized I've got a long way to go. It takes more strength to walk away at times than it does to fight."

Judy puffed a weary breath. "Are you going to walk away, leave again?"

"No. I'm here to stay," he said, calmer now. Resolved. "But I might have to walk away from having Ava Jane back. I won't force things with her. If she doesn't want me then I have to find a way to accept that. But I'm not leaving again."

"I wouldn't give up completely on winning her back," Judy said, taking his hand before he could make it to his seat. "You might have scared her today, but you also came to her rescue. I know the *real* you and today was just a part of the goodness inside your heart. You meant well. She'll realize that after she's had time to absorb what happened. If she still cares, she won't be able to deny that you had the best of intentions even if you did lose control."

"Yes, but she might also realize that she doesn't want anything to do with me because she saw a side of me I've tried so hard to hide. She'll forgive me, Mrs. Campton. But she will never forget what I've done."

"No, but you can't give up on showing her what you can *become*, Jeremiah. God. Remember to talk to God. He brought you home and He'll see you through. God is never quite finished with us, you know."

Jeremiah didn't understand how she could be so sure of that when her own son hadn't come home in one piece. His remains were buried in the cemetery up the road but he was in heaven now.

How did she do it? How did she maintain such a solid, sure faith?

"Thank you," he said, instead of asking her that question.

"You can come to me anytime you need me," Judy said, lifting off her chair with wobbly dignity.

Jeremiah took her arm and allowed her to walk him to the door. "I appreciate you taking the time to talk to me."

She stopped at the open door where Bettye stood smiling at both of them. The loyal housekeeper and all-around helper took good care of the Camptons. Mrs. Campton nodded to Bettye and then walked out on the long, wide porch with Jeremiah. "I wish you'd consider going to counseling, Jeremiah. If you truly want to get through this and find some peace, it might help to talk to someone who is trained in dealing with PTSD."

Jeremiah wasn't ready for that again. He'd gone through some counseling after he'd recovered from his injuries, but he'd never been able to open up to anyone. It didn't sit right with him to bare his soul to a stranger. But wouldn't that be better than losing control the way he had today?

"I'll think about it, I promise. Right now, I have to get back and finish my tasks."

"Come back to see us," Judy Campton said. "And, Jeremiah, you'll be in my prayers."

"And you in mine," he responded, meaning it.

He'd finish his work and then he'd try to find Ava Jane and see if she'd calmed down. Maybe she'd listen to him now.

Or maybe he'd already lost her forever.

"Are you feeling better now?"

Ava Jane woke up to find her mother standing just inside the bedroom door. "Mamm, what are you doing here? What time is it?"

Martha came and sat on the edge of the bed.

"It's almost four in the afternoon. I came because your sister was worried about you. You never take to your bed in the middle of the day, not when you have so much baking to do."

"I'll get to it. I'll stay up late." She tried to sit up, but her body felt weighed down. "I… I had a headache."

The dull ache pulsed throughout her system and hit her right in the heart, while the scene there on the street played out like a bad dream. "I need to take care of the *kinder*. I slept right through them coming home from school."

"Deborah is playing stickball with them," her mother said, pushing her gently back down. "You've been working too hard. No wonder you got a headache. Always happens when you overdo it." Martha touched a hand to Ava Jane's forehead. "Or when you're fretting about something."

"I need to see—"

"Ava Jane, stop."

Recognizing that mother's voice, Ava Jane sat up and slid back against the wooden headboard. "I'm sorry. I'm okay. I drank some chamomile tea and my head is better now."

"Your sister told me what happened. She ran to the phone booth and got word to me to come soon."

"I was okay. I am okay," Ava Jane said, the sound of her children laughing outside the open window bringing her both joy and pain. "I just felt a bit dizzy after…after that man bothered us and…"

"After you witnessed Jeremiah attack the man."

Ava Jane blinked and stared into her mother's eyes, then burst into tears. Bobbing her head, she said, "Yes. Yes. I've never seen anything like it. He looked so angry. Such rage. And it scared me much more than what that Englisch did. It's like I never really knew him at all. Why, Mamm? Why does this hurt so much?"

Her mother gathered her into her arms and rocked her, patting her head and whispering into her ear. "You are in shock. You lost your husband and the man you tried to forget has come back. It's enough, daughter. More than enough to give you a headache. But I think your heart is hurting, too."

Ava Jane cried into her mother's apron, remembering how Deborah had hurried her to their buggy. Seeing Mr. Hartford standing there with worry on his face, hearing him ask if he could do anything to help. She'd seen the Englisch group moving on down the street, that one man turning around to glance over his shoulder. Scared. He'd been scared.

And he should have been. Jeremiah looked ready to tear his head off. She couldn't think past that image because her mind went to places she didn't want to take it. Places of war and pain and death and destruction.

Jeremiah had seen those places, had done that very thing to other men. Had probably killed other men.

She didn't know how she could feel this much hurt for someone she didn't want in her life. How she could pray so hard to get another person out of her system.

Today, she'd seen what he'd become. How could he ever return to what he'd left behind here when he still had such rage inside his heart?

But she's also seen something else after he'd let the man go. She'd seen the genuine anguish and regret in his tormented eyes. Yet, she couldn't forget the darkness of his anger.

Finally, her mother held her up and stared at her, her gentle expression full of compassion and concern. "You hurt because you love, daughter. I think you never stopped loving him."

"No, I loved Jacob. Only Jacob." Ava Jane shook her head but, inside, her heart screamed the truth.

She did love Jacob. Would always love him. But she loved Jeremiah, too. And that scared her more than anything. No one could ever know that. And Jeremiah would never see that. Because she wouldn't show her feelings again.

Chapter Ten

Jeremiah sat near his father's bed. He'd volunteered to stay here today with Daed so his mom and sister could attend the festival in town. They had quilts and other items to sell—pot holders, pretty appliquéd clothes and other knickknacks they'd worked on since the last festival.

They needed the fresh air and light.

And he needed this solitude to keep his mind steady.

He'd come so close the other day to finding Ava Jane and telling her how sorry he was, but after talking to Mrs. Campton and then going back to finish up his work, he'd run into Mr. Hartford.

"Ava Jane and her sister went home after the ruckus. I told the sheriff about those kids. Always coming through here after the high school lets out. They like to tease the Amish. I ran 'em off the other day and I called the sheriff after what they did today." Patting Jeremiah on his arm, he had added, "I, for one, am glad you confronted them. Teach 'em to respect people."

Jeremiah heard all of that and wished he'd handled confronting them in a more peaceful way. "And Ava Jane? Was she all right when she left?"

Mr. Hartford gave him a sympathetic stare. "She was upset. Her sister took her home. I salvaged what I could of her breads and muffins but most of it got crushed and had to be thrown away." He shrugged and looked toward the road. "You know, she gets these bad headaches when she gets upset. Might want to give her a while before you try to talk to her."

Jeremiah came back to the present, remembering how she used to cry from the painful headaches. He couldn't forget how helpless he'd always felt when the pain would overtake her.

He felt that same helplessness now.

He'd stayed away. He couldn't add any more to her pain.

"I'm here, Daed," he said in a shaky whisper. "I've sent the women out for the day. Just you and me."

He'd given the day nurse the day off, too, since Derek had mentioned how his family loved to go to the festival. Derek had three children and a wife, who also worked at the hospital.

His father shrank into himself with each passing day. No hope. But Jeremiah hoped anyway. So he started talking.

"I made it to BUD/S—Basic Underwater Demolition/SEAL training. I knew it would be tough and my instructors made sure I knew it. They never teased me about my background, but I knew they were aware of it every day and reminded all of us that we would belong to them for the next six months. Many weeks of preparations—orientation, they call it. In case any of us might change our minds. Some did. Some just up and quit—DORs, Drop on Requests. I couldn't do that. I'd already given up everything so I toughed it out. I prayed a lot. All the time. I had to run for miles. I had to exercise on an obstacle course. Ironic, that, since we all had our own obstacles to overcome if we wanted to succeed. We had to be healthy, in top shape, so we worked all day long. Healthy in body and mind."

Jeremiah stared at his father and then glanced out at the foot-tall cornstalks. He had the window open to let in the fresh air. The swish of the cornstalks moving in the spring breeze made a nice lullaby. So peaceful, so comforting.

"My instructors figured my toughness came from all the hard work here on the farm. Swimming was the hardest. But I was gifted with loving the water and so I relished swimming, even two miles in the ocean, even loaded down with gear. Edward taught me how to do that, in that big pool at his house."

He stopped and took a breath. "I never knew what that would come to mean to me. I had a lot of resolve, a deep commitment, but there were times when I longed to be right here, sitting by the fire with you and Mamm."

He wanted to touch his father's hand, but shame kept him from doing it.

"That was our first phase of intense training. We all got pretty cocky and overconfident, but then we had to face what they call Dive Phase." He put his hands together, his elbows on his knees. "It's all about oxygen and spending most of your day emerged in water with a rebreather.

"A rebreather. I think that's what the good Lord is giving me right now, because sometimes when I look at Ava Jane I can't breathe.

"You're okay hooked up to the oxygen but the instructors don't let you enjoy that. They tie up your hose and take your regulator away and make sure you come close to drowning. That's when you really find the Lord, Daed."

His father sighed and let out a breath.

Jeremiah stopped, the memory cold and foggy in his mind of sinking to the bottom of the pool.

That sensation of giving up overcame him with a frozen clarity. That floating against a weight so heavy he thought he'd never take another breath. His hands fighting against the knots, fighting against the weight, fighting against gravity and water and pressure and depth.

Jeremiah heard his father's staggering sigh while his own held breath caught against his throat like a chain, holding him back, holding him down. Drowning him.

He had to break free.

For a moment, he was back in that pool, his life flashing before him while he struggled to stay in control. He could see Ava Jane, see the tears in her sky blue eyes and remember the pain on her face the night she'd begged him to stay.

For just that instant, he wanted to push up and out of the water, to find the air he needed to breathe. He wanted so badly to come home. Just come home.

"Jeremiah?"

He turned to find Beth standing there, staring at him.

"Are you all right?"

Jeremiah stood and gulped in air. He hadn't even realized he'd been holding his breath. Glancing down at his father, he wondered how long he'd been sitting so stiff and cold, sweat beading on his brow.

And he wondered if he hadn't already been baptized. But by fire, not water.

Ava Jane smiled at the people milling past the booth she shared with her mother and sister. "We've had a *gut* crowd, for sure," she said, happy that the weather had cooperated.

The booth was full of baked goods, knick-knacks and all kind of handmade items. Pot holders and aprons lined up one side while quilts lay folded for display on a big table on the other side. The smell of meat grilling wafted on the crisp breeze that filled the afternoon air.

Mamm had walked down the long alley of colorful booths to visit with friends, leaving the two of them in charge. Now they sat on stools and nibbled at the lunch they'd packed, enjoying a quiet moment before the next round of customers showed up.

"Ach," Deborah replied, her smile as bright as the sun. "And it's wonderfully *gut* to see my sister having fun for a change."

Ava Jane slapped at Deborah. "I know how to have fun."

"But you'd forgotten."

Seeing the seriousness behind her sister's lighthearted banner, Ava Jane pretended to straighten the already-straight row of banana, pumpkin and blueberry breads she'd made. The row was growing smaller as the day wore on. The oatmeal and full-grains had already sold out.

"I'm okay," she told Deborah. Two days ago, she'd been at one of the lowest points in her life. In pain both physically and mentally, she'd almost made herself sick.

But prayer and lots of talks with her parents and the bishop had helped her grow determined and strong again. She'd get through this. The bishop had given her some good advice.

"These things take time, Ava Jane. Jeremiah has been through a lot and he has come home for more reasons than he's admitting. Mostly, he came home to heal," the bishop had said.

That would take time, considering how he'd reacted the other day. And considering how she'd reacted to him.

She had not seen Jeremiah since that day.

Thankful for that, she wondered if he'd leave her alone as she'd demanded in her shock and anger. She wasn't proud of how she'd reacted but she didn't want to ever go through that again.

"Forgive," the bishop had advised her. "If he confesses his sin before the church and becomes baptized, we will speak of this matter no more."

The bishop had also given her some other advice. Advice she wasn't sure she could follow.

"It's understandable to think fondly of Jeremiah and also to hold resentment toward him. You knew him in childhood and were close to him. You are alone now. He is alone, too. But let nature take its course. Jeremiah has a lot of healing to do and he has come home to do so. Let him heal and then you can consider whether you want to be a friend to him or not. Meantime, forgive him, Ava Jane. Forgive him so you can have some peace, too."

She might not speak of Jeremiah's sin again but she'd always think about him and what they'd been through. Now she had to decide if she could ever get past her own pent-up resentment and anger and learn to tolerate his presence here.

"Don't go getting glum on me now," Deborah said with a twirl of one of her bonnet strings. "We've at least two more hours. Aren't you hungry? You didn't eat much of your chicken salad sandwich. Or maybe you'd like some more lemonade?"

"I had the sandwich an hour ago," Ava Jane reminded her sister. "And in case you haven't noticed, I have food all around me."

"But you can't eat up the profits."

Laughing at Deborah's antics, she looked

up to see her friend Leah strolling through the booths. Leah had sewn and crocheted some of the items in their booth, but with six children the woman barely had time to make clothes for her family and she couldn't help man the booth. But she crocheted beautiful bibs, baby hats and blankets. She kept saying one day she'd open a shop and call it Leah's Triple B Designs.

"Hi, Leah," Ava Jane called out, waving.

"Hello," Leah replied, two children in tow and her youngest in her arms. "Josiah has the other three," she explained. The other three were older and self-sufficient—two boys and the oldest girl. "I came to check on my items, but I have to buy some of that good fruit bread you make, Ava Jane."

"We have your favorites left," Ava Jane said, motioning to Leah to come over. "And I have one apple pie left. I know it's Josiah's favorite."

Leah hurried across to the booth. When she got there, Deborah took the babe in her arms and began to coo and sing to the little girl. One day she'd make a fine mother.

"Thank you for selling my wares for me," Leah said, noticing her pile of various hand-made items had gone down considerably. "I can really use the income."

"Your things are very popular," Ava Jane said, straightening the little blankets, memories of her own children at that age comforting her. "We have enjoyed representing you."

Leah kept an eye on the other two children and then turned back to Ava Jane. "I heard about what happened in town the other day. That must have been terrifying."

Ava Jane steeled herself. But there was no way around it. "It was, but then sometimes the Englisch go out of their way to torment us, don't they?"

Leah looked confused and then nodded. "*Ja*, but it's even worse when one of our own reacts with anger."

Shocked, Ava Jane realized everyone would have heard about Jeremiah's reaction, too. Lifting her spine, she nodded. "He did overreact. But he also came to our defense."

"I'm glad he did," Leah said in a low voice. "Sometimes I wonder if slapping a cheek might work just as well as turning the other cheek."

"We aren't to do that," Ava Jane said, praying she wouldn't do that right now. Leah meant well but no one knew how much this had affected her and she wanted to keep it that way. "But sometimes we do have to bite our tongues, right?"

Leah paid for her bread and pie and nodded. "Right." Then she put a hand on Ava Jane's arm. "You know, I have an opinion regarding you and Jeremiah."

"Everyone does," Ava Jane said on a dry note while her heart pumped faster. No point in trying to stop her friend from giving that opinion.

"It's simple," Leah said. "You're a widow and he's unmarried. You cared about each other once. What's to stop you from doing that again?"

Ava Jane gasped. First the bishop had hinted at this and now one of her friends. "There is a lot to stop me," she said, lowering her voice. "He joined the Navy and fought against others, took up arms. It goes against everything I've ever been taught. It goes against our beliefs."

Leah grabbed one of her rambunctious children and reeled him in. "But we are to forgive him," she stressed. "He wants that. Josiah says Jeremiah is trying very hard to make things right."

Leah's husband was a kind, hardworking man with a big family. He wanted everyone to have the same.

"I know he's trying," Ava Jane said. "I wish everyone would stop telling me that. I'm trying, too. Trying to accept that he's back to stay, trying to accept that Jacob is gone. Trying to see the good and the right in all of this."

Leah's brown eyes widened in distress. "I did not mean to upset you. I'm sorry."

Ava Jane looked over at her friend, realizing

she'd just overreacted again when she'd told herself she would not.

"It's all right. I'm dealing with Jeremiah in the only way I know how. Prayer."

Leah nodded and was about to respond but when she heard a crash and saw one of her sons running away, she shook her head. "I have to go but... Ava Jane, if you ever need to talk—"

"I know where to find you," Ava Jane said, forcing a smile.

Two hours later, while she was packing up tablecloths and the few leftovers, she looked up into the setting sun and saw the silhouette of a man walking up the street.

A strong man with broad shoulders and a steady, solid gait.

Jeremiah. Walking right toward her.

Chapter Eleven

Jeremiah watched her face for signs of fear.

Ava Jane appeared tired and nervous, but he didn't see any fear. More like a steely determination and resolve. She was much braver than he'd ever been. And much more forgiving. He hoped she'd forgive him yet again.

Deborah came around the booth and greeted him with a hands-on-her-hips pleasantness. "Jeremiah, what are you doing here?"

Glancing around, he saw others staring. What did they think of him? Would he ever fit in again, even after they'd forgiven his sins?

"I'm here to help with cleanup. Beth came home to sit with our father, and the home health-care nurse is there with her."

"That's *gut* then," Deborah said, her head held high. "Beth is a devoted daughter." Dropping the defense mode, she added, "Most of the crowds have come and gone and we had a fairly good turnout. Sold a lot of our baked good and other items." Staring down her nose at him, she added, "We hope to have a good end to the day."

Jeremiah ventured a glance at Ava Jane and then back to Deborah. "Are you warning me? Or trying to stop me?"

"Both," Deborah replied without skipping a beat.

The annoying little sister he remembered had turned into an annoying grown woman. With spunk.

Jeremiah turned to where Ava Jane stood behind the protection of the booth. "Do you want me to leave?"

She gave him a troubled stare, her heart in her eyes. He saw the answer. She wanted him to leave Campton Creek. Period.

"No," she finally said. "You did volunteer to help out. We're about to go home anyway."

He nodded and moved away. Then he pivoted back. "I'm sorry," he said, glancing between Deborah and her. "I apologize for my actions the other day. I've been away for a long time and I'm learning things all over again. I hope you will forgive my angry outburst."

Deborah went back inside the booth with Ava Jane but had the good sense to busy herself with packing up the remaining items.

Ava Jane rubbed her dainty hands down the front of her apron, two bright spots of color on her cheeks showing her discomfort. "You should work on controlling that anger you've brought back with you. Or at least let it go. But I wonder how you'll do that. You were trained to become an angry man, weren't you?"

Only she had the power to bring him to his knees with her curt, calm words. "No, Ava Jane, I was trained to be a fighting man, to attack any enemies and to do my job to the best of my ability. I had to learn to stay in control all the time."

She folded up towels and put tablecloths into a basket before turning to face him. "But that requires violence, doesn't it? Which is why you're probably out of control now."

Her words might be harsh but the guarded worry in her eyes told him everything. She *was* afraid of him, of what he might do if he lost his temper again. But he also saw a trace of tenderness there in her shimmering stare. She wanted to understand but how could she even begin to understand how much he'd endured?

"War is violent," he said. "I did what I was trained to do, and while I'm not proud to admit I had to use violence at times, I am proud that I protected this country that shelters us and allows us to practice our religion in our own way."

"Even though our beliefs dictate that we are

not to raise a hand in violence, that we are pacifists and peacemakers, not fighters and killers?"

He took a long breath before he answered. She was a smart woman and she'd obviously somehow studied up on what being a SEAL meant. He would not lie to her. "Yes, even so. I went against our beliefs because, at the time, I felt this need to do something, to fight an unseen enemy in honor of a friend. But I'm done with that now. I came back here. Of all the places on earth, I came home. Because I needed to be here. Right here. And I will work until the day I die to prove that I'm returning to our ways and our beliefs and God's word."

Ava inhaled a breath that sounded like a sob. "Sister?"

She turned her head toward Deborah. "I'm fine. Go and load the buggy please."

Deborah hurried out toward where the buggies were parked and placed some of their items inside. Then she found a friend and started chatting in her animated way, but she kept glancing back toward the booth.

Ava Jane kept busy, her lips pursed and pinched, a soft frown marring her smooth forehead. Her hand stilled on a baby bib appliquéd with blue butterflies that matched her eyes. "Did you kill people, Jeremiah?"

That question threw him. Swallowing hard,

he closed his eyes, images of death surrounding him. "It was kill or be killed."

She went still her eyes wide. "So you did?"

He nodded, keeping his eyes on her. "I took lives, yes. It can't be changed. I can only ask for forgiveness and…learn to forgive myself."

"And what if you can't?"

He couldn't answer that so he began to ask his own questions. "What else is there then? Do I leave again and become the outcast forever? I don't want that. I wouldn't be here if I didn't mean what I say. This is much harder than anything I endured out there."

"Harder than fighting and killing?"

"Nothing can ever be that hard, but I was hoping maybe to find some kindness in your eyes and your words. That's the hard part about facing you—seeing the condemnation you feel for me."

She stared at him, her own anger simmering beneath her sweet, tormented face. "Why did you decide to come back?" she asked, her tone numb and quiet. "Beth said you were in California for a while before you returned here."

"I was," he said, coming around to help her with the baskets of wares that needed to be put away. "When my last tour of duty was over, I was afraid to return home. A coward, that's what I'd become. I did my time and left the military, and then I landed in California since that's where I'd started my training. I worked on the farms out there. Produce for miles and miles. Fields of fruit and rows of olive trees, almond trees and grapes that would make wine and jam and juices. I loved being out in the fields and being in a clean, calm place near the sea."

He thought about that vast ocean that he'd fallen in love with, thought about the crashing waves that he'd learned to maneuver. Sometimes late at night when he couldn't sleep, he'd remember that cool water flowing over him like a soothing balm.

Pushing away those memories, he continued. "But I missed home. I missed my family. And even though I knew you were married, I missed you and Jacob—and my life here. When Beth mailed me and said our father was dying, I took that as a sign that I needed to return."

Ava Jane's eyes held his but he couldn't read her thoughts. She was as closed off to him today as she had been for all these many years. Even way back, she'd always held a part of herself away. He hadn't minded it so much when they were young. But now it shouted at him loud and clear. He'd lost her. Or maybe he was just now seeing what he hadn't seen back then. Maybe she'd never been his at all.

"I have to tell you something," he finally

said as he lifted a basket and started walking with her toward her buggy, glad at least that she didn't push him away. "I'm not going back out there. I am here to stay, receive my baptism, confess *all* of my sins and give my life over to the Lord. If you can't stand the sight of me, I will stay away from you. If you can't forgive me, I will accept that and I promise I won't bother you again. If we pass on the street, I will look the other way to save you the discomfort of speaking to me."

Setting the basket in her buggy, he turned and faced her again. "And if you can't forgive me, Ava Jane, I will understand and it will hurt for the rest of my life, more than any wounds I've suffered, but I'll have to learn how to handle that."

She stopped near the buggy, her surprised gaze full of questions and yet, she said nothing.

So he continued while he still had the strength.

Touching a hand to his forehead, he said, "One good thing I learned in the Navy—I learned how to focus and concentrate on what needs to be done, to block out all distractions. I'll do that here and probably for a long, long time. I am disciplined and I'm in good shape. Maybe I'll find a wife and settle down and have babies and finally be a happy man. Maybe. But then that wouldn't be fair to any woman I married because I'd always be pining for someone else."

Then he leaned close. "I will always be near *you* and I guess I'll have to take that as all I'll ever have of you. Just being near you. It will have to be enough."

He turned and left before he started begging her, before she could respond with more measured words. He wouldn't look back. He would not force her to see what little good he had left in him. If she found any good in him, it would have to be through her own actions and her own eyes. And the seeing and forgiving would have to come from within her heart.

Because he was badly wounded, in both spirit and in physical body, and not yet strong enough to force anyone to do anything. If she ever came to him, he wanted her to come of her own accord and because, at long last, she wanted to be with him again.

She almost called after him, but her sister's hand on her arm stopped her. "That was some show you two put on."

Ava Jane held Deborah's hand. "It wasn't a show. It was as if we were the only two people left in the world." She stared after Jeremiah, her heart hammering in her chest with such an intense pain she almost doubled over. "And I think this will be the last time Jeremiah ever bothers me. I've lost him for good this time."

"Lost him?" Deborah frowned and got into the buggy seat. "Did you ever have him?"

"No," she said, lifting up to sit beside her sister. "I meant I've lost a chance to at least be a friend to him. I haven't understood him at all and I never will. Looking back, I don't think we truly knew each other at all, even before he left. I'm not a very good Christian now because I'm having a hard time forgiving what he did. What he became." She inhaled a breath to keep from sobbing, but her grief would always be twofold. "He implied I'm a distraction and that he will ignore me from now on."

"You are the best distraction he's ever had," Deborah said, taking the reins as they headed toward home. "Don't let him do this to you."

"He's not doing this," she admitted. "I'm doing it to myself because I've wrestled with this since he left me. Now he has solved my dilemma. He has decided in his own way to shun me, to save grace and keep me from being uncomfortable, and I can't blame him. I've been horrible to him. He's taken the hint and he says he will stay away from me. So I won't have to fret about Jeremiah Weaver again. It will be as if I never existed for him."

He'd find someone else. Several of her single friends had eyed him outright at church. He didn't mean that part about never being able to marry another woman. "He'll move on now," she managed to whisper. "And I'm glad for it."

Deborah's derisive snort echoed out over the gloaming. "We'll have to see how that works for the two of you."

"It has to work," Ava Jane said. "We are both here and we can't avoid each other. But we can pretend to ignore each other and that means I won't have to deal with him in any personal way, at least."

"This is going to be hard for both of you from what I've seen," Deborah pointed out. "Campton Creek isn't big enough for the two of you trying to avoid each other."

But Ava Jane would do her best to avoid Jeremiah. And she knew, after today, he'd do his best to stay far away from her.

She'd hurt him.

Which brought her to the other nagging thought now centered in her mind. What kind of wounds had he suffered in fighting for his country? And would his wounds every truly heal?

Chapter Twelve

She'd spent the last two weeks trying to ignore Jeremiah Weaver. But the man seemed to pop up in the oddest places.

He always had business at the general store and Mr. Hartford didn't have a clue that Jeremiah and Ava Jane were at odds. Jeremiah had been long gone when Mr. Hartford inherited the store from his parents ten years ago. And besides, the kind Englisch man was not one to gossip or make observations. He respected the Amish. But he seemed determined to shove any single Amish man and woman together. So Ava Jane had taken to checking each aisle and even the hardware and lumberyard out back before she ventured past the produce section.

True to his word, Jeremiah did not approach her, even on the one day she came close to bumping into him. Before Mr. Hartford could gather them into his conversation, Ava Jane had taken off in the other direction.

But she saw Jeremiah's furtive glances and frowning expressions.

She'd stopped two days ago with her children in the pretty park just past Campton House, hoping to give them a few moments to walk the trails and enjoy the warm day. The park had exploded with new fronds on the tall pines and green shoots on the budding oak trees. A weathered white gazebo stood at the center of the park and held a perfect view of the water and woods. Nearby, a dogwood promised to burst forth with white blooms.

It was peaceful and quiet until she looked up to find Jeremiah walking along one of the winding, tree-shaded trails. He kept his head down, his hat drawn low, probably because he didn't seem to like bringing attention to himself. He hadn't even looked their way.

But she knew he was around. Always around. She'd noticed his buggy going up and down the road in front of her property. A buggy that never stopped in her yard.

He did work hard. She'd give him that. Beth went on and on at their last frolic about how he'd painted the house and cleaned out the barn and repaired everything that creaked or squeaked.

"He sits with Daed every morning and every

night," Beth divulged to the fascinated group of women who'd gathered at Leah's big house. "Sometimes I hear him talking about...things... he did out there. Sometimes I hear him praying."

Praying. That notion had brought Ava Jane's head up and got her heart beating too fast. She'd never pictured Jeremiah praying. Not since he'd left, at least.

The man was a paradox. Too confusing for Ava Jane to understand.

Now another Sunday had rolled around. As she worked with the other ladies to serve dinner since the church service was over, she watched with a shuttered gaze as Jeremiah helped with putting out chairs and moving tables and then assisted elderly Mrs. Knepp to a shaded bench underneath a towering oak.

When he turned, he caught Ava Jane staring and immediately hurried the other way.

In spite of the cool afternoon breeze, Ava Jane's skin burned hot. He was truly shunning her. No, avoiding her. Ignoring her. Hurting her.

As you've done to him. But she'd tried so hard to be kind and forgiving. Hadn't she?

Remembering the minister's message of doing unto others, she lifted her chin and continued with her work. Easter was coming, a day of resurrection and new beginnings. She'd be kind and civil to the man. If he ever looked at her again.

The weather was wonderful on this Sunday. One week before Easter and two weeks before Sarah Rose's seventh birthday. She could focus, too. *She* hadn't gone through some sort of rigorous physical training to do so. Ava Jane had her faith and the disciplines she'd learned from the Ordnung to train her in the ways of the church.

So why was she having such a hard time focusing these days? Why did it hurt that Jeremiah's beautiful smile was so rare? That his blue eyes looked so cloudy and tormented? That he walked among them as a man who'd gone cold and numb, tortured and stoic?

"He swaggers."

She whirled to find her friends Hannah and Leah glancing from her to Jeremiah. "What?"

"Jeremiah," dark-haired Hannah Smith said, her prim smile full of curiosity. "He swaggers. It's like he walks differently from most of our men. Have you noticed?"

Why did her friends always ask her to define Jeremiah? Had she noticed? *Yes.* His swagger was one of the things about him that both scared her and intrigued her. He moved in a way that showed too much confidence and made him too masculine. He might be world-weary and tired, but Jeremiah was still a handsome man.

A dangerous, handsome man.

"He's so different now," Leah said, adding to Hannah's remarks. "But then, I only remember him as a boy. He was always as cute as a button and stocky, but now…" She shrugged. "Josiah says it's the warrior in him. Might be hard to get rid of that."

Why was Leah so interested in this? Ava Jane's older friend usually didn't abide gossiping and ogling. Now she was discussing Jeremiah with her husband? Had Josiah warned her to stay away from him?

The warrior. Yes, she'd seen that warrior side of Jeremiah. And she was trying sorely to avoid him and his swagger.

"I haven't noticed," she told her fascinated friends before she hustled to put out tea jugs and then went to her buggy to get the three apple pies she'd made.

Just as she reached for the long flat woven basket holding the pies, two boys ran by and almost knocked her off her feet.

But a strong hand grabbed her before she lost both the tray of pies and her footing.

Her gaze on the long basket tray, she struggled to balance and said, "Thank you." And then she looked up and into Jeremiah's midnight blue eyes.

"You're welcome," he said, taking the basket right out of her hands. "Boys."

Her heart did the bump-bump that made her lose her breath. "Boys will be boys." She checked to make sure her Eli hadn't been in the unruly group.

"Remember when that was us?"

His quiet words touched her and stung her.

"You aren't supposed to be speaking to me or assisting me," she reminded him, a deliberate nip of chill in her words.

"I'm going to take these pies to the table over there," he said, indicating with his chin toward where several other desserts were already being displayed. "I wasn't trying to bother you. I just happened to be passing by."

Then he nodded again and hurried to deposit her load before he headed back inside the big, roomy barn where they'd held services for two hours.

So he *was* good at ignoring her, Ava Jane thought with a trace of despair and disappointment. She'd return the favor by not looking his way again.

No, she hadn't noticed Jeremiah or the changes that only made him more attractive and intriguing. She hadn't noticed his dark unruly hair or the scars on his hands and…one tiny crescent-shaped scar near his left temple.

Nor had she noticed how he walked or talked or breathed.

Or prayed.

Not at all.

Jeremiah ate his meal in silence, the banter and easy conversation of the men around him only making him stand out even more than he already did. They treated him nicely enough but he didn't offer up much in the way of conversation, which made some of his old friends glance at him with uncertainty and maybe a little bit of judgment.

But he could handle that.

He'd learned how to make himself invisible. To blend in and sit so still that people would start talking over him and around him and through him. So he'd watch and listen and learn a few details that would help his team down the road. Details that could save lives.

Right now, he was keen on hearing the details of Eli Graber planning to sneak down to the creek with his friend Simon Kemp.

"My *mamm* doesn't like it when I go swimming. She's scared of the water," Eli said from the spot away from the table where he and Simon had clustered. "My *daed* drowned there and it makes her sad. It makes all of us sad. We miss him."

The other boy's fascination caused his freckled face to go blotchy. "That's a terrible way to die."

Eli nodded, his dark eyes so like Jacob's, casting up to make sure no one was listening. "Yes. It was bad. She won't even teach Sarah Rose how to swim. That's why I have to sneak down to the creek. Daed taught me. He said his best friend taught him. I'm pretty good. I'll show you."

Jeremiah remembered sneaking down to the creek with Jacob, remembered showing his friend how to hold his breath and go under. Ava Jane would find them and sit up on the bridge, because, for modesty's sake, girls weren't supposed to swim with boys. She'd been terrified of the water anyway.

Jeremiah took a breath and pushed the memories away. He missed Jacob, too. Why did his friend have to die there of all places?

Another irony between them that Jeremiah couldn't explain. Why had God given him such a keen love of water and made Ava Jane so scared of it, only to have her husband and his friend, Jacob, drown at the very creek where they used to hang out?

His father had taught him how to swim, telling him he'd never know when that ability might come in handy.

An understatement. And yet another irony. His father, whom he loved dearly and who now did not want Jeremiah in his house.

Jeremiah kept listening, just to silence all of his questions. It wasn't up to him to stop the boy. Ava Jane wouldn't like him interfering. But she wouldn't like it if Eli disobeyed her either.

Jeremiah lifted up off the bench without making a sound and casually walked past the boys, a solid smile on his face.

"Good day, Eli, Simon. What are you two cooking up over here?"

Guilt colored both of the boys in shades of red that matched the checkered tablecloths.

"Uh, hello, Mr. Jeremiah," Eli said, his gaze shifting out over the crowd. "We were talking about the creek."

Surprised that the boy had been honest, Jeremiah nodded and glanced off in the distance where he could see the water from the Bylers' hillside farmstead. "It's one of those spring days where you want to get your fishing pole out and bring home a nice trout or a mess of perch. You two thinking about going?"

Eli glanced at Simon. "Maybe. Either that or…swimming." He almost said something else but halted, his mouth shutting into a grim line.

"Water's still a bit chilly," Jeremiah said. He'd never admit he'd gone swimming since he'd been home. Usually late at night or early in the morning when no one was out and about. He also knew how to slide through the water without even making a splash. "Might want to wait a few more weeks."

"How do you know that?" Simon asked with a daring, shrill voice, accusation in his eyes.

Eli held quiet but looked as if he had a lot he wished he could say.

"I stuck my toes in," Jeremiah replied, leaving it at that. "Besides, you know how mothers can be about little boys sneaking away without permission. I'd think long and hard before I went swimming. Maybe talk to your *mamm* first."

Eli's eyes went dark with disappointment. "She does not like the creek."

"She has good reason," Jeremiah replied, giving the boy a steady stare. "You wouldn't want to hurt her feelings now, would you?"

"Eli!"

They all three whirled to find Ava Jane standing there with her hands on her hips, glaring at them. "Stop sputtering and help me load the buggy. It's time to go home and do chores."

Simon whirled and ran away while Eli stared at Jeremiah in obvious wonder and then stalked toward Ava Jane. She said something to him and then marched over to Jeremiah.

"So, you decide to avoid me but you manage to talk to my son? What was that all about, Jeremiah? More questions about guns and curiosity about your former life? Trying to turn my son into something he can never be by influencing and encouraging him?"

Hurt that she'd even consider such a thing, he shook his head. "That's not what it was about."

Her eyes wouldn't let go of their doubt. "Then what?"

Jeremiah wouldn't squeal on Eli. The boy had got the message. No need to fill her in on things. "That was boy stuff. Sometimes young boys need to talk to older men about things. We talked about fishing and swimming once the water is warm. Your son is interested in that, nothing more." Watching her confused reaction, he added, "And as far as I know, those are normal things that all young boys like to do."

He nodded to her before she could respond and then turned and headed home on foot. His sister had come to the service with a friend and his mother was home with his father.

Jeremiah needed some time alone to think about how much the effort of trying to avoid Ava Jane was exhausting him and confusing him.

Did she want him around?

Or was she just playing a game of her own

to punish him and make him suffer before she finally allowed him fully back into her life?

Either way, his patience was running thin. He'd have to refocus and pray even more for the Lord to give him the strength he needed to keep his eyes on the prize. That prize would be God's grace. With or without Ava Jane's blessings.

Chapter Thirteen

"Ava Jane, you have a note here from Mrs. Campton."

Ava Jane whirled at Mr. Hartford's comment, her gaze falling on the fancy cream-colored envelope he held up.

"Are you sure?"

"Got your name right here in black ink," he said with a soft smile. "Her assistant person left it yesterday."

Ava Jane took the envelope and rubbed a finger over the scrolled lettering. "Someone has lovely handwriting."

Mr. Hartford nodded. "The Camptons do everything first-class."

"Yes, they sure do," she replied, careful to place the envelope in the pocket of her apron. "*Denke*, Mr. Hartford."

Hurrying away, she gathered the few items

she needed and made sure she'd placed the money Mr. Hartford had given her for this week's supply of baked goods inside her other pocket.

No sign of Jeremiah, thankfully. But each time the bell on the door of the general store dinged she half expected to see him standing there. Even her weekly trips to this old-fashioned country store had been tarnished by memories of Jeremiah.

And from seeing the man himself here in front of her.

Still smarting from their encounter at church two days ago, she remembered having a talk with Eli yesterday.

"Why do you insist on talking to Jeremiah Weaver?"

"I don't, Mamm." But her son's eyes shone bright and he didn't look her in the eye. "I mean, not unless he talks to me. He's always kind to me."

"You don't know him."

Eli finally faced her, his expression pinched and guarded. "But you did. And so did Daed. I know he's the one who taught my *daadi* to swim."

Suddenly it all fell into place. Eli wasn't fascinated with Jeremiah because of where he'd been. He only wanted to know more about the man who'd been so close to his daddy.

"Who told you that?" she asked, her heart breaking for her boy. What kind of tales were people telling?

"I heard some of the men talking. Heard how they used to run around together and swim in the creek and hunt with Daed and Mr. Jeremiah. Is it true?"

"Yes, it's true. But that was a long time ago."

Eli's brown eyes went rich with unshed tears. "Is that why you get upset when he's around? 'Cause you miss Daed?"

Gathering her son into her arms, she'd kissed his unruly hair and said, "*Ja*, I get all emotional and want to have a good cry because of the memories and because I loved your father so much."

Then her son had asked yet another hard question. "Then why don't you like his friend?"

She hadn't been able to give a good answer to that one. "I like him. But he's been gone a long time so I have to get to know him better."

"So you don't want me to talk to him?"

"I want you to be careful when you talk to all adults."

She wished she'd done better by her son, but here she stood with yet another reminder of all the ways Jeremiah Weaver had betrayed her and his faith.

She'd open the note from Mrs. Campton when she was alone back home. Ava Jane hurried about the store, grabbing her needed items and tried once again to forget about Jeremiah. She only saw a couple of people in the store and when she headed to her buggy parked in a designated spot in the lot beside the store, it looked as if she was one of few people out and about today.

The main street through the town, aptly named Creek Road, was nearly deserted. So she loaded her basket into the buggy and guided Matilda toward home, glad for the solitude.

Taking the buggy out onto the main road, she thought again about seeing Jeremiah at church. He'd looked good. Healthy and settled, some of the strain she'd noticed on his face a few weeks ago now replaced with a quiet reserve and a solid resolve. He'd always been stubborn and single-minded. He must truly be focusing on getting back right within the church. He didn't converse with the other men a lot, but he spoke when spoken to and he helped as needed. Now and then, she'd glance his way and actually see him smiling at a comment someone had made.

Jeremiah had a beautiful smile.

Urging Matilda on up the road, Ava Jane silently reprimanded herself and tried to find something else to occupy her mind.

Her mother and Deborah had come by early this morning to check on her, a sure sign that she was giving off some sort of distress signal.

"Any more headaches?" Mamm asked, concern in her question. "You were quiet at services on Sunday."

Ava Jane ignored that remark. She'd tried to stay busy after church. "No. I'm better. That last one was a doozy."

"You haven't suffered headaches in a while," her mother noted. "Remember to take care of yourself. Drink your chamomile tea and get some rest."

"I'm fine," Ava Jane replied. As fine as she could be, considering.

Deborah flittered around the spotless kitchen, picking up fruit and studying the contents of the cabinets. "I remember the bad attack you had after Jacob died. Understandable, of course."

Ava Jane barely remembered much from those dark days except the piercing pain inside her heart, but thinking about it gave her muscle memories of pain and despair all over her body and brought out a hazy dread inside her soul.

To lighten things, she asked, "Is that why you're both staring at me as if I have bugs crawling out of my *kapp*? Are you still concerned that I won't be able to handle things?"

"No," Deborah replied. "You look fairly normal this morning. You've always handled things just fine."

Ava Jane smiled at that. "I function most days and I'm okay, really. I think the worst of it is over."

"You mean the worst of having to accept Jeremiah being back in the community?" Mamm asked, her voice soft with compassion.

Ava Jane poured coffee and got out her notebook. "Yes. We've reached a truce. We don't even notice each other anymore."

Her sister snorted and her mother frowned.

"That might be for the best," Mamm said while her frown turned to a neutral expression on her still-young face.

"Yes," Ava Jane agreed. So why was she so riled about it? She almost told them about finding him talking to Eli, but decided she'd given everyone enough fodder regarding her and Jeremiah. Instead, she added, "So let's change the subject and get down to the business of planning Sarah Rose's seventh birthday party."

Her mother and sister had the good grace to leave things at that, but she knew her family was worried about her. Daed came by most afternoons to check on her. Knowing how blessed she was to have such a loving family, she didn't begrudge them. Right now, they brought her comfort and kept her grounded.

Today the sun was bright on her garden so after she unhitched the buggy and took care of Matilda's needs, she went to work on hoeing weeds and pruning tender shoots. Her spring flowers were already blooming. Petunias, daisies and lilies colored the many groupings she'd worked on. Soon, she'd have tomatoes, onions, peas and beans and herbs in the little vegetable garden behind the house, too.

Bending over, she noticed something fluttering out of her pocket. The note from Mrs. Campton. She'd forgotten about it.

Ava Jane stared at her own name on the elegant paper, too many bitter memories warring inside her brain. What could Edward Campton's mother possibly want with her? And why such a formal way of reaching out to her?

Shoving the note back into her pocket, she finished up with her garden work and then washed her hands and made herself a quick dinner. The *kinder* would be home soon and, after hearing about Jeremiah's conversation with Eli last Sunday and then having her own talk with her son, she planned to take them for a walk down to the creek. It was painful to go there, but her children were getting older and more curious about their father and his death. She wouldn't bring it up unless one of them asked. But they should know their father and keep him in their memories. Maybe going there would help with that, at least. And she'd take Eli back to fish there, too.

Because seeing him seek advice from Jeremiah rubbed her the wrong way. It shouldn't. Her son was seeking answers she had not provided. She'd do better at that.

Thank You, Father, for allowing me to see this need.

Jeremiah had been the one to point it out.

Thank You, Father, for allowing me to see that Jeremiah has some good traits.

She cleared away her dishes and then settled in a rocking chair with a cup of mint tea. Finally, she pulled the now-crumpled note out of her pocket.

Dear Ava Jane,

I was wondering if you'd come by to see me sometime this week. My husband's seventy-fifth birthday is coming up and I'd like to celebrate with a cake. I've sampled some of your baked goods from Hartford's and so I'd like to hire you to bake the cake. But we need to talk about what kind and

such things. Can you come by on Wednesday morning?
Sincerely,
Judy Campton

Ava Jane didn't trust the Camptons. She knew they were good people but…they'd taken Jeremiah from her. How could she do this? Go and take a food order from a woman she didn't care to associate with?

You could use the money.

That was true. Judy Campton's influence stretched far and wide around here. Ava Jane might receive more orders from this one visit. Was she willing to do that? To go and talk to Mrs. Campton? The woman hadn't done anything to her and she knew the Camptons had been generous to the Amish community their ancestors had allowed to settle here. They'd lived together in peace for centuries and this generation could be the last of the Camptons, but one part of her wanted to ignore the formal request.

Manners dictated that she should visit the elderly woman. Mrs. Campton didn't venture out much these days. She seemed to prefer staying close to her husband, who had been in ill health for months now.

It would be rude not to show up, wouldn't it?

At least, she shouldn't have to worry about seeing Jeremiah there.

The next day, Ava Jane wore her best blue dress and a clean white *kapp*, her hair caught up in a bun underneath, her white apron crisp and fresh.

"Do you want me to wait for you?" her father asked, questions coloring his hazel eyes. Her father never brought up the subject of Jeremiah Weaver, but his need to protect his daughter shouted through his stoic silence.

"Why don't you park and go sit on that bench out in the front garden?" Ava Jane said. "I'm sure Mrs. Campton won't mind that."

"Will she mind if I fall asleep with the bees humming around me?" Daed asked with a teasing grin.

"She probably won't even notice." Ava Jane patted her father's sturdy arm, noting the fatigue that seemed to shadow him these days. "I won't be long, I promise."

Her father gave her a gentle gaze full of love. "If you need me…"

"I'll be fine, Daed."

Knowing he was nearby did bring her comfort.

She didn't know why she'd asked her father to bring her here, but she felt safe with him and she knew he'd intervene on her behalf if anything about this meeting upset her. Because Ava Jane figured this summons was about much more than baking a cake.

Nerves tingling like the silvery wind chimes she saw hanging on the rambling white-columned front porch, Ava Jane stood staring at the massive black front door. She'd never been to this house. Jeremiah had always wanted her to see it. Odd that now she was finally here.

Made of red bricks and trimmed in black shutters, the house welcomed with transoms over the heavy door and windows. Georgian style, she'd heard it called.

She lifted a hand to the brass door knocker and then waited for someone to answer, her heart beating like a trapped bird inside her chest. Ava Jane almost turned around to leave but the door creaked open before she could escape.

"Good morning." Bettye Byer, the widowed housekeeper who'd also become an assistant and lived on the estate since her husband had passed away twenty years ago, greeted Ava Jane with a welcoming smile.

"*Gut* day to you," Ava Jane said. "It's *gut* to see you again, Bettye. I hope you found lots of buys at the spring festival."

"I did," Bettye said, guiding Ava Jane inside

where a marble floor shimmered in the morning light. "I told Mrs. Campton she should get you to bake the cake for Mr. Campton's party. The blueberry pie I brought home went pretty fast."

Feeling more at ease, Ava Jane smiled. "I'm glad you enjoyed the pie and thank you for recommending me."

"Let's get you into Mrs. C's sitting room before she wonders if I've kidnapped you and taken you straight to the kitchen," Bettye said with a wink.

It was rumored that Bettye had once been Amish until she'd met an Englisch man and married him. They never had children, but because he was the caretaker of Campton House and took care of the expansive gardens, they'd lived here in the carriage house.

Romantic, but Ava Jane's hurt cut through that notion.

Jeremiah had been in this house, had enjoyed the graciousness that Bettye was now showing her. She had to stop thinking about that and concentrate on why she was here.

Ava Jane straightened her clothes and followed Bettye, noticing the other woman's gray bobbed hair and her creamy skin. Bettye looked young to have been around so long. Maybe her attitude made her seem carefree, but Ava Jane wondered what she'd sacrificed by leaving her family and faith to marry someone forbidden.

She prayed that Bettye and her husband had been happy here.

The house was impressive. Not as fancy as she'd imagined but comfortable and full of antiques and beautiful artwork. She passed a mirror and was shocked to see her own wide-eyed image there.

"Here we go," Bettye said. "I'll bring out some refreshments for you two."

She showed Ava Jane a cozy little room off the back of the house. "This is the sunroom. Mrs. C likes to sit here and read most mornings."

"Denke," Ava Jane said, glancing to where Mrs. Campton sat smiling over at them.

The room was filled with sunlight that glistened off the white wicker furniture and shot back out into the massive backyard, spreading all the way to the creek. She noticed a small dock with a rowboat nearby.

Out in the yard, old camellia bushes bustled together like ladies at a church meeting and massive azalea bushes held fresh pink-and-salmon-hued buds that reminded her of quilt scraps. Beautiful.

But when she glanced to the left and saw the huge pool, her mind shifted back to the task ahead. She needed to get this over and done with.

"Ava Jane," Mrs. Campton said, holding out a hand. "I was afraid you wouldn't come." She patted the floral cushion of a high-backed wicker chair next to her own. "Please have a seat. I would stand to greet you, but it takes me too long to get up."

"Hello," Ava Jane said, sitting down on the edge of the chair. "It's good to see you, Mrs. Campton."

"I doubt that," the woman said, laughing. "I would imagine this is the last place on earth you'd want to be."

"You'd be right about that," Ava Jane said, surprising herself. "I almost didn't come."

Judy Campton gave her a shrewd once-over. "This house held bad memories for you even before you entered it."

Since the woman seemed intent on getting to the bottom of things, Ava Jane nodded and took her time glancing around at the potted ferns and exotic houseplants. "I don't really know much about this house or you," she said, her voice calm in spite of her sweaty palms. "But Jeremiah holds you in high esteem."

Judy Campton's green eyes met hers with a focused appraisal. "He holds you in high esteem, too. That's why I thought it was time for us to meet."

Anger caused Ava Jane to sit up, her spine stiffening. "I didn't come here to talk about Jeremiah Weaver."

"No, we're here to discuss cake," Judy replied, her gaze never wavering. "But we'll get to that. I just wanted to meet you, dear, because... well...my husband and I won't be around forever. It's important to us that Jeremiah has someone he can turn to if he needs help."

"What do you mean?" Ava Jane asked, surprised yet again. "Is he ill?"

"Not in any physical way," Judy said. "But he's hurting inside. He gave up a lot to do what he did."

"I'm well aware of what he gave up," Ava Jane replied, keeping her tone kind.

"Then you should also be aware of what he might one day suffer, even more than he already has."

Now the woman had her worried. "What are you trying to say to me?"

Bettye came in before Mrs. Campton could reply. Carrying a tray complete with two floral-edged china cups and a dainty teapot, she set it on the oval table between them. "Tea and some snack cake. Not as good as yours, Ava Jane, but one of Mrs. C's favorites. Spice cake."

Ava Jane didn't think she could eat a bite of the dark pecan-crusted snack cake. Why did this woman bring her here?

And what was so wrong with Jeremiah that Mrs. Campton would demand that Ava Jane needed to know?

Chapter Fourteen

"What do you mean?" Ava Jane asked, her teacup halfway to her lips.

"Have you ever heard of PTSD?" Judy asked, her own tea forgotten on the table.

"No." Ava Jane put the delicate china cup and saucer down and stood. "I have to go. I'll be happy to bake your husband's birthday cake but you can have Bettye send me the details."

"Please," Judy said, trying to stand. "Don't go."

Ava Jane saw the worry and remorse in the woman's aged eyes and immediately guided Judy back into her chair and then sank down on her own. "I can't talk about Jeremiah. I won't."

"All right," Judy said. "I'm so sorry. I've said more than I intended. But he still cares for you and… I feel I need to warn you."

Ava Jane's heartbeat accelerated as she took

in a deep breath. "You mean, to warn me about the anger he's holding inside, the kind he displayed on the street the other week?"

Judy nodded, clearly as rattled as Ava Jane. "I'm divulging subject matter that is very personal. I don't normally interfere in such things, but I love Jeremiah…like a son…and I deeply respect what you've had to deal with, too."

Feeling contrite, Ava Jane leaned forward. "I'm sorry. But you brought me here under false pretenses."

"No, I really do want that birthday cake. Bettye and I both are getting too old to spend a lot of time in the kitchen." Judy finally took a sip of her tea. "It's just that when I saw you I couldn't help but blurt that out. Someone needs to be aware."

Ava Jane took another breath and decided to listen to the woman's concerns. Curiosity and fear gave her the grace to do so. That and her burning need to understand Jeremiah. "Is he a danger to himself or others?"

"No." Judy Campton shook her head. "Not unless he is provoked by someone meaning to do harm. Did he tell you he was badly wounded?"

Ava Jane put a hand to her mouth, horrible images crowding her head. "No, but I've wondered."

"Jeremiah is a hero," Judy continued. "My

husband doesn't have all the details, but he asked around and found out that during a mission that went bad, Jeremiah saved two of his team members and several civilians, even though he'd been shot. But something happened that he can't get over. Something he's locked inside himself. That's the thing that makes him angry sometimes. When he sees injustice of any kind, he reacts."

Ava Jane held her hands together, remembering how even growing up Jeremiah was always the first to defend those he loved. "The way he did with those young people. He was protecting my friends and my sister." She looked up at Judy. "And me."

"Especially you," Judy said. "When he came here right after he attacked that man, he was so shaken. I've seen it many times. Post-traumatic stress disorder is something that a lot of military men and women go through. Those who've been on the front lines suffer it the most. I have volunteered for many years at a nearby clinic where members of the military go to get help. I've encouraged Jeremiah to talk to the counselors there."

A clinic. Ava Jane had been only once to the big hospital about thirty miles away, when a distant family member had been ill. This clinic must be connected to that facility.

"But he refuses?" she asked Judy, her heart breaking apart.

"For now," Judy said. "I think he'll change his mind on that one day. I pray."

"Are you asking me to *not* provoke him or *to* protect him?"

"Neither of those things, dear," Judy replied on a soft note. "I'm explaining to you why he might lose his temper at times. He has flashbacks that can cause nightmares or cause him to withdraw. If I'm guessing correctly, he probably feels uncomfortable in a crowd, standoffish and silent. What I'm telling you has to remain confidential, but I think Jeremiah will recover with care and nurturing and some counseling. But, Ava Jane, he needs a friend."

Ava Jane put her hands in her lap, the image of Jeremiah standing away from the other men at church front and center in her mind. "And you think I should be his friend. Me, the woman he left to go and put himself through that kind of torture? You think I'm the one to help him heal when he and I can barely be near each other. He knows how I feel. I resent him going away and I resent him returning here. I can't get past what he did, even though I know in my heart I have to find a way to forgive him."

Judy nodded, her eyes misty and full of understanding. "You're the only one who *can* calm him and help him to heal," Judy said. "I'm only asking you because I know how he feels about you. He was devastated the other day after he went after that misguided young man."

Ava Jane felt drained and even more concerned for Jeremiah. Only, she didn't have the strength to help him. "Thank you for telling me these things, Mrs. Campton," she said. "But I can't be responsible for healing Jeremiah. He will have to find a way to do that himself."

"Just consider what I've told you," Judy said, insistence in her voice. "Jeremiah is a good man. A kind, hardworking man. He needs his family and his community in his life, especially because of his emotional wounds."

Ava Jane wondered about that and tried to steel herself against feeling anything more than being sorry for him. "I needed him in my life," she said. "But he chose to leave me."

"Greater love has no one than this, that someone lay down his life for his friends," Judy said, her words floating out over the room in a whisper.

John 15:13. Ava Jane knew the verse.

She closed her eyes and fought back the tears. "Hasn't he given enough?"

"More than enough," Judy said. "That's why he's come home."

Ava Jane sat silent for a few moments. "I will

do my best to be kind to him and to watch out for him. But I can't become involved with him, do you understand?"

Judy nodded, shrewdness bringing color back to her eyes. "Yes, I'm beginning to understand so much more than I ever did."

Bettye walked in, right on cue. "Did you two decide what kind of cake we need?"

Judy gave Ava Jane a reassuring glance. "My husband loves carrot cake. Could you do a three-layer one with cream cheese icing?"

Ava Jane nodded, afraid to speak, amazed at how Judy Campton switched from an intense conversation to a lighthearted order with a blink of her intelligent eyes.

But finally she said, "I'd be glad to bake the cake. My father favors carrot cake, too."

"Then you should bring him to the party," Judy said. "In fact, I'd love to have you here at the party to help us serve. I'd pay you for your time, of course."

Feeling a bit put off, Ava Jane didn't want to come back to this house, especially since she might run into Jeremiah here, and she certainly didn't want to be bribed into working in this house. She had to make that clear. "I don't usually take on that kind of work. I have two children."

"I've insulted you," Judy said. "Bettye, help me to keep my mouth shut from now on."

Bettye shook her head and gave Ava Jane an apologetic smile.

"I'm not insulted," Ava Jane said. "My friends have mentioned working for you. I'd just prefer not to."

"Then come as my guest," Judy said, leaning forward. "I think you and I could become good friends."

Ava Jane didn't see that happening either but she finally let go of a smile. "Are you always this persuasive?"

"Yes, she is," Bettye said, laughing.

"Let's get that cake baked," Ava Jane finally said. "We'll let God take care of the rest."

"Good idea." Judy sat back and sipped her tea, a proud smile on her face.

Bettye told Ava Jane when they'd need the cake and gave her the time of the party. This coming Saturday afternoon. "You can deliver it earlier that day or we can pick it up."

"I'll pay extra if you deliver it," Judy added. "We don't drive very much anymore either." Then she grinned at Ava Jane. "Maybe then I can convince you to stay for a while."

"I thank you for the invitation," Ava Jane said, getting up to really leave this time. "I'll bring you the cake but I don't think attending the party would be wise on my part."

She turned and headed out of the room before Judy Campton could talk her into anything else.

"What took so long?" Samuel asked when she came rushing down the front steps.

"Too many cakes to make a rash decision," Ava Jane replied. "And too many cooks in that kitchen."

"Ach," her *daed* said with a soft smile. He didn't ask for any further explanation.

As they left the Campton estate, Ava Jane sent up a thankful prayer for her father's solemn quiet. She couldn't talk about what she'd heard at Campton House. But she could double up on her prayers for everyone involved, including herself and Jeremiah.

She needed prayer now more than ever.

Jeremiah had been wounded out there. Wounded by a gunshot and still he'd apparently saved others.

And he'd lived. He'd survived for a reason.

Dear Lord, thank You for bringing him home.

That unexpected prayer surprised her, especially when she realized she'd been in denial for weeks now. A gentle thankfulness filled her spirit and this time she didn't push it away.

If he hadn't been wounded, how long would he have stayed and fought? For a lifetime? She might not have ever seen him again.

That brought up a new revelation. She became glad in her *heart* that he'd made it home. Glad she'd had this second chance with him, to forgive him in person.

Too glad at this moment.

She didn't understand why that notion made her want to cry happy tears right along with her sad tears, but she had to blink to clear her eyes.

Had she been denying her true feelings for Jeremiah? Or were *these* feelings new and fresh and different because they were both changed and different now?

"You're mighty quiet," her father said as he clicked his tongue for Matilda to move along.

"I've got a lot on my mind."

"More than cake?"

"A lot more than cake," she said with a soft laugh that didn't ring sincere.

"You'll figure it out, daughter. You're smart, you know."

She wondered about that. Judy Campton was the smart one. Because she'd opened up that tiny hole in Ava Jane's heart and flooded it with compassion Ava Jane hadn't wanted to feel, and had made her see the truth she'd been trying so hard to deny.

Jeremiah had come home to stay. But he'd brought a lot of that world outside of Campton

Creek with him. Would he ever be able to let go of what he'd been trained to become?

And would she ever be able to let go of what she'd built up in her mind, the bitterness and resentment and unbreakable hurt of being rejected by the man she loved?

"Daadi," she said with a weak whisper, "your oldest daughter needs a lot of prayer."

"Daughter," Samuel said in return, glancing over at her briefly, his eyes full of compassion and love, "my oldest daughter is prayed for every day."

Ava Jane patted her father's arm and then looked out over the rolling hills and green valleys of spring.

A new beginning.

Maybe it *was* time to let go of the past.

Saturday morning, Jeremiah was back at Campton House helping to set up tables and chairs underneath a big catering tent. He'd been invited to attend the Admiral's party later today but had decided not to do so.

He was no longer part of that world, a world where he'd made money and put it in a savings account in case his family ever needed it, a world where he'd had to wear a dress uniform at times, his gold trident insignia shining brightly while he greeted high-ranking officers and politicians. A world where he'd watched two of his eight team members die on the battlefield.

Because he couldn't save them.

He'd let the Admiral enjoy his seventy-fifth birthday without having to endure the elite members of Campton Creek's social scene gawking at the Amish man who'd joined the Navy and was now home.

SEALs didn't like attention. They were trained to ignore honors and accolades and publicity. Secretive and covert, that's how they lived.

Now he wanted that but in a different way.

He wanted to be left alone with his family and his faith.

With his thoughts of the woman who could never return his love. A different kind of war raged inside his soul now.

And in hers, too. She was fighting against what they once had together because he'd left her and broken her heart.

He deserved her scorn and her condemnation.

But, oh, how he wanted, needed her love and forgiveness.

When he looked up from his work to find Ava Jane standing on the big back veranda of the house, staring down at him, Jeremiah wondered if he was having one of his dreams.

But when she waved and gave him a shy smile, he became fully awake and aware. So he walked toward her with a tentative smile of his own.

"What are you doing here?" he asked carefully.

"I baked the birthday cake," she said, her smile tight now and unsure. "I should have known you'd be helping out with the celebration."

No condemnation. More of a quiet resolve.

"Just setting up and taking down later. I seem to be a jack-of-all-trades and a master of none."

"You are a hard worker."

A compliment. He'd take it.

"I like to stay busy and I like this kind of work. Where I don't have to splutter along or make small talk."

Holding her hands together against her crisp white apron, she watched him as if she were seeing him for the first time. "Like we're attempting to do right now?"

He laughed at that, a sound of relief in his own ears.

"Are you speaking to me again?"

She nodded, something new and fresh in her gaze. "Yes." Then she came down the steps and stood a few feet away. "This is a lovely place. A peaceful place."

He couldn't deny that. "*Ja*. Quiet and se-cluded, pretty."

"I can see why you were drawn to it."

"But you're wondering why I keep coming back?"

She shook her head. "No, I'm beginning to understand, I think. Whatever happened to you here, Jeremiah, is now part of you. I'm truly try-ing to accept that."

He didn't dare break this tentative thread by asking what she meant by that statement. Could they be civil? Friends? More? "It's good to see your smile, Ava Jane."

She smiled again. "I must go. I brought the cake by while Mamm and Daed are at their house with the *kinder*. I hope the party goes well. I'm sure you'll be here so I hope you'll taste the carrot cake."

He couldn't take his eyes away from her, even when he saw Mrs. Campton watching them from the big bay window with unabashed in-terest. "No, I'm not attending. I'll visit with the Admiral later, when things are quiet." Then he grinned. "But I will tell Bettye to save me a slice."

Ava Jane moved a bit closer, her gaze flash-ing on the other workers around them. "Does it bother you then, to be around a lot of Englisch? A lot of people?"

He held tightly to a heavy white plastic chair, his knuckles almost the same pale white, because he didn't dare move toward her. "It bothers me to be around people, *ja*. But I can make an exception to that whenever *you* want to be around *me*."

She lowered her head and gave him that precious smile again. "I've been thinking about that. We have to find a way to be friends, Jeremiah. Everyone deserves a *gut* friend, don't they?"

He didn't want to hope because he wasn't sure they could stay *just* friends. "What made you change your opinion on that?"

She didn't answer right away. Instead, she put her hands into the pockets of her apron. "A lot of prayer and some wise advice from someone who made me see beyond my pain and judgment."

With that she turned and stared up at Mrs. Campton, gave her a wave and then hurried around the corner where the open gate let workers in and out.

"Ava Jane?" Jeremiah called after her.

She whirled at the gate. "Yes?"

He swallowed, then took in a gulp of air. "I could use a friend."

Nodding, she hurried away.

Jeremiah watched her go and then stared up

at Judy Campton. The woman wore a serene smile, as if all was right in her world.

Jeremiah was left to wonder just how much that birthday cake had cost both the baker and the taker.

Chapter Fifteen

Easter morning.

Jeremiah sat with his father, his mind on the last week. "I've finally started feeling at home, Daed," he said. "Ava Jane has…changed. She's back to smiling at me and actually talking to me. She wants to be my friend."

Of course, that could go the other way in a hurry. He'd prepared for that but he was trying to be respectful about reining in his fighting side, about not allowing his anger to overcome this new mission. Would he always have to be careful around her? Around the entire community? Would he be able to let go of his nightmares and truly find peace?

"A couple more months before I confess all and go before the church to be baptized," he said now. "I've met with several of our leaders and told them I'm committed to returning for good.

Eighteen weeks of training." He shrugged. "It's a lot like my SEAL training but more of a mental thing than physical. Although I've poured myself into learning the eighteen articles of the *Dordrecht Confession of Faith* in the same way I learned stamina in basic training."

During those meetings, Jeremiah had told the ministers some of the details of what he'd seen and done, but he had yet to open up to anyone other than his sleeping father. He'd been reading his Bible, as he always had, and they'd discussed the Ordnung with him, bringing him up to speed as his buddies used to say.

Now he understood why Edward Campton had felt safe in telling Jeremiah about being a SEAL. While Edward had never divulged top secret information, he had poured his heart out to Jeremiah. Because he had known he could trust him to never repeat their conversations.

Edward had been a godly man, a true believer. And he'd also believed his work was important. But he'd suffered greatly because of that work, too. Edward had never complained to his parents, but he'd given up a lot to be a good SEAL.

Jeremiah understood that same suffering now. He could talk to his dying father because no one was around to judge him.

"We had eight team members," he began.

"And we all had nicknames. We were based out of Coronado, California. So I was called Amish, of course. Our commander was Mudbug, because he was from Louisiana. Then we had Rider—he loved motorcycles—and Cowboy from Texas; Peanut—Georgia; Broadway Joe—New York; Hillbilly—Tennessee; and Gator from Florida.

"All good men. Strong men who gave it all to our missions. We trusted each other, although I had to earn their trust, you know. But once they saw I was all in, they had my back."

Jeremiah stared into the dawn, remembering other dawns, dark and dangerous and filled with smoke and heat, the smell of an acrid burning and the ear-piercing boom of an explosion.

"Remember how I used to love to run around and play with pretend guns and make-believe horses? Where did that come from? Why did I have this dark streak inside me? Why did I have to go away and become a machine instead of a man?"

His father sighed in his sleep. Now and then, he'd mumbled but never opened his eyes. His father's silence echoed out over the muted light from the kerosene lamp on the bedside table. Jeremiah had learned how to bathe him and change his soiled clothing, and he'd learned how to change out the feeding tubes that sustained his father's last days on earth. Thankful that he had the money to hire more nurses if needed, Jeremiah remembered happier times with his *daed*.

One of those times had been at Campton House, building and creating beautiful things for a family who had now become a part of his life. His father had conversed with the Admiral and Mrs. Campton and even Edward. They'd all laughed together.

But those good times could never be again.

Now Jeremiah said his usual morning prayers and then took a deep breath. "Gator and Cowboy didn't make it home alive."

He had to stop, to catch a hand to his stomach. That sick feeling hit him every time he thought about his two friends. And those women and children. He'd saved a lot of people that day, but he'd lost two people he loved dearly. And some people he'd never even known.

Collateral damage. Innocent human beings in the wrong place at the wrong time.

Unable to tell his father about that horrible day, he stood and wiped his eyes. "That's all I've got today, Daed. Some things are too hard to speak about."

With that, he went into the kitchen to start

the coffee and do what he could to help with breakfast.

"How many times have I told you that's my work?" his mother said when she came in from the little room she'd been sleeping in to be near her husband.

Jeremiah turned as she fussed with her bonnet strings. "I know it's odd, Mamm, but I've learned to fend for myself even in the kitchen. I don't mind helping wherever I'm needed."

Moselle stared at him in the same way she did every morning, as if she couldn't believe he was actually standing in her kitchen. "So much has changed through the years. You're all grown up and handsome and your sweet *daadi* is at the end of his days. I wish…"

Jeremiah knew what she wished. "Me, too," he said. "But I'm here and I'm not leaving again. *Sie Batt nemme duhn ich gern.*"

He would willingly take his father's part.

And he could see now what was eating at him and keeping him awake at night. He needed forgiveness for what he'd had to do in the name of duty. He needed forgiveness for leaving. He needed forgiveness for not being here to help his family and for Ava Jane. How could he ever accept that forgiveness when he didn't think he deserved it?

"I thank God for your return," his mother said

as she busied herself with scrambling eggs and frying ham. But then she turned back and hurried to him. Putting a hand on his cheek, she said, "God's way, Jeremiah. God's time."

Then she went back to her work. Jeremiah felt something new and warm inside his heart. A touch of humanity, a touch of hope. His world brightened and the morning light shifted and poured through the lacy kitchen curtains like a stream of clear water.

Beth stumbled into the kitchen and hugged Jeremiah tight. "Happy Easter, brother."

"Same to you," Jeremiah said, noting her pretty dress and fresh *kapp*, his heart suddenly full. "How are things with you and Joseph Kemp?"

"What things?" Beth said with a warning glare and a glance at her mother.

"She's pretending," their mother said from her spot in front of the stove. "Joseph doesn't know it yet, but the rest of us do. I predict a proposal by summer's end."

"Mamm," Beth said with a giggle. "We are just friends."

"If you say so," her mother retorted. Then she eyed Jeremiah. "I know several single women who have inquired about my son, too."

Beth's eyes widened in surprise. "Really now? Most of them seem to run the other way." Her teasing giggles sounded like the wind chimes Mrs. Campton kept in her garden, dainty and tinkling.

Jeremiah couldn't deny he'd encountered some curious women since he'd returned home. They wanted a husband and he was as good as any to them. They had no idea. No idea at all of the kind of baggage he'd bring into a relationship. He thought of Ava Jane and knew he needed to stay away from her for that reason, if nothing else.

"I'm not looking," he said now, his words too sharp.

Both his mother and his sister turned to stare at him, shock and worry in their gazes.

"I'm not looking," he said again on a gentler note. "I think I'll remain a bachelor all of my life."

"I wouldn't count on that," his mother said, her knowing eyes going soft as she relaxed again. "You will make someone a fine husband one day, I pray to God."

Beth's glance shifted from her mother to Jeremiah. "*Ja*, and we all know who that someone might be."

Jeremiah grabbed some coffee and a ham biscuit and headed out the door to do chores. But he stopped on the porch steps and watched as the beautiful pink-and-salmon dawn crested to the east over the trees guarding the big creek. The sun's rays shot out in a golden slumber that left him breathless and hopeful.

He closed his eyes and felt the warmth of that rising sun on his skin and bones and imagined Ava Jane walking toward him, wearing a wedding dress, a sweet smile on her face.

When he opened his eyes, the sun was still there but the dream disappeared in a mist of reality. And off in the distance, gathering clouds promised rain on the way.

Too much to hope for.

Too hard to imagine.

He'd have to settle for being her friend. That way, he could at least watch out for her and help her if she needed him. *If* she needed him.

Draining his coffee, he went about his work so he could clean up and head to church.

To be near God's grace.

And to be near the woman he wanted in his life forever and yet couldn't have.

"Eli, straighten your shirt."

Ava Jane fussed with her son's clean clothes and tried to tidy his dark hair. While the Amish didn't go all out for Easter, they still celebrated with a big meal and lots of fellowship. They'd had a somber Good Friday and a quiet Saturday and now, church on Sunday. Then tomorrow would be Easter Monday—more food and fellowship and family time.

In spite of the upheaval of having Jeremiah back over the last couple of weeks, Ava Jane accepted him more and more each day. But while they had developed a tentative friendship, she knew she had to avoid anything else.

So that meant she couldn't wake up thinking about him or wonder during the day how he was doing.

"How does my hair look, Mamm?" Sarah Rose asked, her long golden ponytail peeping out from her Sunday *kapp*.

Her daughter was growing up so fast. "You look pretty," she said, adjusting the ponytail a bit. "And your dress is just right."

"I like the blue," Sarah Rose said. "I can't wait to hide Easter eggs after services."

"That's always fun," Ava Jane replied, taking a deep breath. She'd see Jeremiah today. That would be her Easter treat for the day.

Then she shook her head and chastised herself again.

"Mamm, why are you shaking your head?" Eli asked, his lip jutting out. "I tucked in my shirt and straightened my suspenders."

Now she'd begun to do odd things in front of her children, too. "Just musing," she replied. "I wasn't shaking my head at you. You look handsome."

"Are we walking?" Sarah Rose asked, ready to go. Her good little daughter seemed so eager to please.

"Not today. Aunt Deborah and Mammi and Daadi are going to pick us up." Glancing out the window, she noticed puffy clouds trying to shut out the sun. "Good thing since the sky can't make up its mind today."

"Can we go outside and wait on them?" Eli asked, always eager to be out of the house doing anything that could get him into trouble.

"Let me gather a few things and then, yes, we'll sit on the bench by the road and wait for our ride."

Ava Jane picked up her basket of cookies and two *snitz* pies, their aromatic mixture of dried apples, oranges and cinnamon wafting out into the crisp morning air. After they did one last check on their Sunday best, Ava Jane and the *kinder* headed down to the corner where someone had long ago erected a taxi bench near the phone booth. Sometimes, the Amish had to use modern means of getting to and fro for work or business in the nearby towns.

The old bench sat weathered and rickety but still sturdy. Ava Jane remembered other times, sitting here with her friends. The boys would run by and pull their hair.

The first time she noticed Jeremiah, really noticed him, she'd been sitting right here. He'd playfully tugged at her *kapp* strings, causing her white covering to go askew and fall right off her head.

A couple of years older than her, he'd seemed larger than life.

"I'm sorry," he'd said, running back to pick up the soiled *kapp*, a broad smile asking her to forgive him. His dark blue eyes had captivated her and her heart had done a funny little dance that day.

The same dance it did now, whenever she saw the man. Or thought about him, which seemed like every time she turned around lately. Why couldn't she get that image of him standing in the garden of Campton House out of her mind? Or the hope in his voice when he'd told her he could use a friend?

Eli's fingers tugging at her dress caused Ava Jane to come out of her musings. "What is it?"

"There's Mr. Jeremiah. He told me he'd take me fishing one day. May I go, Mamm?"

"What?" Ava Jane glanced up the lane and, sure enough, the very man she'd been thinking about appeared over the horizon. Beth sat next to him in the buggy, no doubt on her way to church with him.

"We'll talk about that later," she said to her son, her eyes on the approaching buggy. Taking a breath, she schooled her expression into something she hoped looked friendly.

Eli got up and waved to Jeremiah and Beth. "*Gut* morning."

Jeremiah brought the buggy to a halt, his gaze moving from her son to Ava Jane. "*Gut* morning to you, too. Are you waiting for a ride?"

Ava Jane stood and straightened her skirt. "*Ja*, my parents and sister should be here any minute now." She smiled at Beth. "Hello. How is Ike?"

Beth's blue eyes went misty. "About the same. Mamm insisted on staying there with him and the day nurse."

"We'll send her some food," Ava Jane said, wishing she could do more. Then she looked at Jeremiah, reminding herself of their new truce. "I'm glad you are here with your sister and mother."

"So am I," he replied. Then he smiled down at Eli since her son was hovering near the buggy. "How are you, Eli?"

"Will you take me fishing?" Eli blurted before Ava Jane could hold him back.

Jeremiah shot Ava Jane a questioning stare.

"That depends on a lot of things. First, your mother has to give her consent."

Eli squinted up at her, the crinkles around his eyes reminding her of Jacob. "Mamm? Is it okay?"

Ava Jane's heart became at war with itself. She could be friendly to Jeremiah, but did she dare let her son grow close to him? "I told you we'd discuss this later."

When she heard another buggy coming up the road, she breathed a sigh of relief. Her parents had arrived.

Sarah Rose and Eli rushed to greet their grandparents while she stood silent and uncomfortable by Jeremiah's buggy.

"What if I went with them?" Beth asked, hope in the words. "You, too, Ava Jane. We could both go fishing with them. I haven't been fishing in a long time."

Jeremiah's serious gaze changed to a bemused half smile, but the steely, daring look in his eyes didn't die down. "Plenty of chaperones, since you obviously don't trust me to be alone with the boy."

"It's not that," Ava Jane said. Turning to gather her basket, she whirled back. "I don't like my children being near the water, is all."

With that declaration, she tried to push the sudden realization and hurt she saw in his eyes away and pivoted toward the buggy where her parents and sister sat, watching the whole interaction.

"Morning," Daed said, his gaze on the other buggy.

"*Gut* day," Ava Jane replied as she crawled inside and onto the back seat where her children huddled with Deborah under the heavy canvas covering.

"Mr. Jeremiah and me are gonna go fishing," Eli announced as her father waited for Jeremiah to go on ahead. "One day. After Mamm and I talk about it more."

Her mother glanced back at her with a raised furrow in her forehead and then turned back around.

Deborah poked Ava Jane in the ribs and whispered, "Is that true?"

"I haven't decided," Ava Jane said. "I'll have to consider that very carefully."

"Well, when you do consider that," Deborah whispered with a giggle, "I'd like to be a frog on a lily pad sitting nearby. Because that would be interesting to watch."

"Yes," Ava Jane retorted, "according to you and a whole lot of other people, too."

Seemed everyone around her was either pushing her toward him or warning her to be cautious. Or maybe they were more afraid for Jeremiah to have to deal with her. After all, she had to be a source of great woe for the man.

Ava Jane sat back on the buggy seat and asked God to give her the strength of friendship.

Nothing more.

She wanted to be his friend.

But what if that could turn out to be the worst thing for both of them?

Chapter Sixteen

The nice Easter day soon turned from partly cloudy to fully dark. The egg hunt was winding down when the first lightning strike moved across the sky to the west.

"Kumm," Ava Jane called to her children as they ran by, looking for colored eggs. "We'd better get home before the storm hits."

Some people had left right after dinner on the grounds of the huge Schofield farm. Now everyone started scurrying when a clap of thunder followed the lightning. The horses neighed and began stomping, their dark eyes wild with anxiety. She hurried to where the buggies were lined up like gray-covered boxes, then turned to look for her parents. Her father was helping someone else and Mamm hurried around, gathering children still out looking for eggs.

Another bolt of lightning clashed through the

gray sky, followed four heartbeats later by a boom of thunder. One of the horses near Ava Jane reared up, his nostrils flaring.

Glancing up, Ava Jane saw the big animal towering over her and reached up a hand to shield her face. She took a step, but the horse shot up again and she gasped, watching as his big hooves hovered in the air near her head.

Before she could move, a strong arm reached out and lifted her into the air. Startled, she whirled as Jeremiah sat her down three feet away and then rushed toward the frightened horse.

"There, there," he said, staying near the horse and slowly reaching out to soothe the animal. "*Gut, gut.* It's okay. Just a bad storm brewing."

His soothing voice soon had the animal calm again. The owner came over and took charge. "*Denke*, Jeremiah."

Jeremiah nodded to the other man, then straightened his dark vest and found the hat that had fallen off his head.

"Are you all right?" he asked Ava Jane, his dark hair curly in the wind.

"Yes, thanks to you," she replied, touched by how he'd handled the frantic horse and the man who had not spoken to him before today. Remembering being in his arms for those few seconds, she swallowed and tried to think of something to say.

"I don't know where this storm came from," he said before she could form any words. "But it is springtime."

"*Ja*, and we'd better get home before we're drenched."

"Today was nice," he said as he walked her back to her parents' buggy. "The service has a new meaning for me now, since I've been back."

"The resurrection is always moving and encouraging," she replied. "Such beautiful music and...knowing that Christ rose again after so much pain and anguish. That he went through that for us."

"He lives, so we can live."

Jeremiah was right, of course. The love of Christ shone through their faith. A deep warm feeling filled her heart, causing the layers of her pain to peel away bit by bit. "I'm sorry," she said, looking up at him.

His blue eyes went as dark as the sky. "For what?"

"For the way I've treated you. It's been confusing, I know."

"Ava Jane, I'm the one who's sorry. I can't begin to tell you—"

A commotion near the big barn caused them

both to turn around. Men were running and a woman pointed to the east.

"Fire!" somebody shouted. "At the bishop's place!"

"I have to go," Jeremiah said, pushing past her.

"*Ja.* Of course." She watched him running out toward the road, where several other men were hopping onto buggies.

"He didn't even take his buggy," Deborah said from behind her. "Where is he headed?"

"Toward the fire," Ava Jane replied, worry suddenly filling her with dread. Running toward danger.

Daed rushed up to them. "He signed up last week for the volunteer fire department."

"What?" Ava Jane held her hands together, a silent prayer moving through her. True to his word, Jeremiah was doing his best to stay on the straight and narrow. But, true to his nature, he still had a need to seek out dangerous work, whether he got paid for it or not.

Daed urged her mother up onto the seat. "Let's get home. I think this one will give rain."

Martha looked toward the plumes of black smoke. "I know we're to stay out of the way, but we need to pray that Bishop King's home will survive this fire."

Ava Jane got into the buggy just as big fat

drops of moisture hit her skin. But she wasn't sure if her wet cheeks were from the rain or the tears now falling down her face. She prayed for the bishop and his family and the firefighters. But mostly she prayed for Jeremiah. He still wasn't completely healed.

He fought against the wind and rain and tore through the billowing, suffocating smoke, his only goal to save Bishop King's barn and stables. The rain helped but the fire wasn't contained yet. Along with a dozen or so other men, some Amish and some Englisch, Jeremiah held up fire hoses, climbed ladders and broke through fallen walls to get to the source of the fire.

A lightning strike.

The smells and sounds shattered the shield he'd built to protect himself, and the shouts held him in a grip of flashbacks that he couldn't run from. So he kept working, harder than the others, fighting against the fatigue taking over his body. He'd pulled the horses out first. Made sure no humans were inside the barn. Now he worked the bucket line and helped the firemen from the nearby fire station move and shift the heavy hoses, water from the pump truck spraying up to meet the fire and the rain.

Everything had to be contained.

"Jeremiah?"

He turned and suddenly realized where he was.

Here, in Campton Creek.

The bishop pulled him away from the wet rubble, his own face smudged with dirt and grime.

"Jeremiah, *kumm*. The fire is put out. You can rest now."

Jeremiah stood, his whole body shaking, and saw the other men staring at him, some with admiration and some with concern.

"I'm sorry," he whispered to the bishop.

"For what? You almost single-handedly saved my place. We owe you a great debt, my family and me."

"You owe me nothing," Jeremiah responded. "I need to get home now."

The bishop wiped at his soot-covered clothes and rubbed his silver beard. "*Ja*, go to your folks. They'll be worried."

Jeremiah started passing through the group of sweaty, dirty men, images of other tired, dirt-covered men assaulting him. Lowering his head, he refused to look anyone in the eye.

"Jeremiah?" the bishop called.

Jeremiah turned. "Yes, sir."

"You are home. You can rest now, son."

He nodded and kept walking, his silent tears leaving streaks of clean against the blackness that covered his clothes and body.

The rain and wind, so violent and unyielding before, now came down in a soft cold drenching that washed him and soothed him.

Almost.

Buggies passed. People waved. Yet another kind soul who at first had stood away from him stopped to offer him a ride.

"*Denke*, but I'm all wet and filthy. I'm almost home."

The man and woman and three teens all smiled at him and moved on.

He was dirty, chilled, soaked and still shaking but a warm spot formed inside his hardened heart. A sense of home filled him, a sense of being a part of a strong community where people looked out for each other. He and his father had helped to build the bishop's big barn over fifteen years ago. It was solid, built by men who knew exactly how to move in unison and make everything fit into place.

Now he'd been a part of saving something he'd helped create.

Is that the way with You, Father? You take something You created and save it over and over again, the way You are trying to save me. I want to be worthy. I need to be worthy again.

A small voice told him he'd always been worthy.

But he wasn't ready to respond to that voice yet.

When he made it to the drive up to his parents' house, he stopped and stood in the rain, taking in the sight of flowers in the mist and white curtains, crisp and clean. The old porch swing squeaked a welcoming melody and the scent of pure, fresh air assaulted him.

And pushed away the dark memories that haunted him so often.

Maybe it was time he stopped fighting. Against himself.

"It was a sight to see."

Ava Jane sat with her parents and some friends who'd come by to visit on Easter Monday, another day of rest before the workweek began again. The Millers and their three daughters along with Deborah's not-boyfriend—their big brother, Matthew—were gathered around Mamm's big table, munching on ham sandwiches and baked potato casserole left from yesterday.

Mr. Miller and Matthew, who kept casting

glances toward Deborah across the table, had seen the fire and gone to help out.

"I'm telling you, that man could move. Jeremiah is a strong one. He got six skittish horses and two milk cows out of that barn, with the roof over his head about to collapse."

"Then he ran back in and called out to make sure no one was trapped inside," Matthew added to his father's story.

"Organized the volunteers, too. And pretty much had things under control before the town fire truck arrived. Impressive, how he saved that barn by thinking on his feet."

Mamm sent Ava Jane a quick glance, probably checking to see how hearing about Jeremiah's heroic deeds was affecting her.

She was all right. She had to be all right. Jeremiah had done a good thing and all the people who'd witnessed it now held him in a higher esteem than they did yesterday before the fire.

He needed that kind of boost and acceptance.

"Maybe he learned some of that while he was away," Matthew offered up. Then realizing what he'd said, he turned red and lowered his gaze. "I mean, maybe he's just smart that way."

Daed, ever the diplomat, cleared his throat and scrubbed a hand down his gray beard. "We have to consider that some good has to come from Jeremiah being away. We don't know how and when that good will appear, but I think yesterday is an example."

"An example of what?" Ava Jane asked, the words hitting the air before she could pull them back.

Daed leaned up and placed his hands together on the table. "An example of the best a man has to give, even after he's been through the worst."

Everyone became quiet for a few moments. Mamm offered more coffee and dessert. Finally, Matthew stood and looked at Deborah. "Want to go for a walk?"

"I'd enjoy that." She looked to her father.

Daed nodded and then gave her the behave-yourself stare.

After they hurried out to the back porch, Mrs. Miller shook her head. "Those two don't even know they are smitten, do they?"

"They are in denial," Mamm said with a soft smile. "Meantime, I'll be saving up material for a wedding dress."

They all laughed at that.

Ava Jane got up and began removing dishes to take to the big sink. Feeling a tug on her dress sleeve, she looked over at her mother.

"Daughter, did our talk upset you?"

Ava Jane cleaned off the dishes, her head down. "I have to accept that I'll hear things about him. And it's been better between us.

We've both made our peace, but I still can't see any good in him going away to fight and harm others."

"What he did changed your life so it's hard to see past that," Martha said, patting her hand. "Remember the good in the life you have now. Your children, your family, people who care about you. You found a way to get over losing him. That hasn't changed."

"But I'm doing that without my husband," she replied, wishing Jeremiah hadn't become such a thorn in her side.

"Do you blame Jeremiah for Jacob's death, too?"

"No. But I have to question where the good is in his dying…when Jeremiah got to live."

Her mother readied the dishwater and took the rag from Ava Jane. "God will show you the answers one day, and maybe sooner than you think. But it is not up to us to question or doubt God's plan. You can't blame Jeremiah simply because he survived and Jacob died."

Ava Jane took that into consideration.

But in her heart she accepted that some things were too hard to bear and there were no answers for this kind of grief and torment. Prayers and reading the Scriptures might help but she'd never truly understand any of this.

She didn't want the burden of blaming others

to weigh her down anymore. She didn't want the burden of the ache in her heart to turn her bitter and hateful.

"Jeremiah did a wonderful thing yesterday," she finally said. "He's courageous and honorable. But it seems there is a part of him that still craves that kind of danger." Then she turned to her mother, tears in her eyes. "He came back to us, but he could have been hurt or killed yesterday."

Martha's eyes filled with compassion and understanding.

"Ah, so that's it then."

"What?"

"You still love him. Even more so now than before."

Ava Jane shook her head. "*Ne*, I do not. I can't."

Martha held her dishrag still but she didn't respond.

Ava Jane could see what her mother was clearly thinking. Her sister and Matthew weren't the only ones in denial around here.

Chapter Seventeen

Jeremiah finished the day's work and headed toward the creek for a quick swim. It would be sunset soon, so no one should be about. Most folks would be retiring inside for the night, for supper and maybe some Bible reading and family time playing board games.

Derek was with Isaac since this was the time of day when his father seemed to slip away a little more with each sunset and the nurse stayed nearby to watch his vitals.

Until Mamm ran him out of the room, too.

"My time with him," his mother had explained to Jeremiah and Beth. "Just him and me, with me doing the Bible reading and talking, but it's precious time to me."

But she made sure Derek was nearby in the living room.

Jeremiah didn't like leaving the house but his

mother probably wanted him and Beth to take some time to themselves, too. Especially Beth. They'd both insisted she go to the singing tonight with the rest of the young people.

And his mother had shooed him away. "Get a nice bath and read your Bible."

So now he stood underneath the bridge at the far corner of the big wide body of water. The long covered bridge had been built over a narrow stream that moved away from the expanding creek and into the hills and woods near his family's property. The red-colored bridge, trimmed in aged brown crossbeams and open underneath the center arch, had been built well over a hundred years ago to allow people a quick way across the water and woods, but a local gardening society had raised funds to preserve it and maintain it. He was pretty sure Mrs. Campton had spearheaded that.

Wearing an old work shirt and trousers, he took off his dusty black boots and socks and walked into the shallows. The water's cold wetness hit him, reminding him of the chilly rain on Easter Sunday. Reminding him of the cold against the heat, the fire against the water.

Things had changed somehow. People waved to him more and smiled at him. Asked him how he was doing, how were his father and mother. What was Beth up to?

Had his family been inadvertently shunned, too, because of him? If so, he'd somehow received a little bit of forgiveness for helping with the fire on Sunday. Even Mr. Hartford had praised him when he'd gone into the store earlier today to pick up some things for Beth and Mamm.

"Heard you saved the day."

"I didn't do anything more than the other volunteers and firemen."

"That's not what I was told," Mr. Hartford had replied with a knowing smile. "I always knew you were a good man, Jeremiah. Now they do, too."

He didn't want to be anyone's hero. Not anymore.

And he remembered the shock in Ava Jane's eyes when he'd taken off to help with the fire. Had he lost her yet again?

He took another step or so into the water, the chill numbing his tired bones. That fire had brought out a lot of emotions but he'd managed to work through them without falling apart.

Before, he'd have had to go somewhere quiet and dark to hold himself close so he could become invisible. The memories and images of war and death would have pierced him like daggers and torn through him with the velocity of bullets. Would have wounded him all over again. But here, he could move away from the brutality that haunted him. Here, he was becoming whole again.

Chest deep in the chilly water, he lifted up and started a long lap across the water, following the bridge to the other shore and then moving back and forth, not bothering to count. He knew the feel of swimming a mile or two.

When he swam, his mind would calm and he'd drift into memories of the good times with his buddies. The laughter and camaraderie, the secrets revealed, the times of doubt and fear where he could at least share his faith with them.

"Pray for us, Amish," one of them had always asked right before a mission. Some were believers, others more skeptical. Cowboy had been a devout, faithful man. He had usually prayed right along with Jeremiah. Then he'd look Jeremiah in the eye and reassure him, "We're doing what we can to make a difference. Remember that."

Had he made a difference? He prayed so. Else, Cowboy and Gator had died in vain.

After several laps, he lifted up to tread water and admire the last of the sun's rays peeping over the trees to the west. Taking a deep, calming breath, he walked up on the bank and sat down, his muscles stretched, the kinks worked out of his joints.

When he heard laughter down the way, his whole body went on alert. Pushing his long, wet hair back, Jeremiah put on his hat and crept up the bank so he could see across the bridge.

Two boys walking toward the middle, carrying fishing poles.

Eli Graber and his friend Simon Kemp. They weren't wet so they hadn't been swimming, but he guessed they'd sneaked off to get in some evening fishing. Not much time left since the sun would be behind the trees in another half hour.

How should he handle this situation? He could sneak away and forget he ever saw the boys, or he could let them know he was here and go up there and fish with them for a few minutes before he made sure they got home safely.

He opted for the second choice. He'd never forgive himself if he left them here and then something happened.

Yes, he had that burden to carry, too. He needed to stay one step ahead of the people he cared about. He didn't want them getting hurt or worse.

"Hey," he called out, grabbing his shoes and heading up the earthy bank. "It's Jeremiah Weaver."

Eli and Simon both whipped around, looking surprised and a bit scared.

"Hi," Eli said before he and Simon gave each other furtive glances.

Then he looked over Jeremiah's wet clothes, his mouth dropping open. "You've been swimming?"

"Ja," Jeremiah said, taking one of the old poles to check it out. "I can help you tighten the cork and put a better hook on this. Did you bring a tackle box?"

Eli shook his head. "No, sir. We left in a hurry."

"Is that water cold?" Simon asked, completely oblivious to being caught in the act.

"It's cool," Jeremiah said, finishing up with what he had on hand to make the pole and line work. "Here, Eli, try this."

"We have worms," Eli said. "Got 'em out behind the chicken coop."

"Smart move," Jeremiah said, watching the sky. "You two cast out and see what's out there and then I'm taking you home."

"You don't need to do that," Eli quickly replied.

"Yes, I do." Jeremiah worked on untangling Simon's line. "Your *mamm* will be worried, unless of course you cleared this with her first."

Eli kept his eyes on the cork floating through the dark water. The boys both went silent.

"I see," Jeremiah replied. "All the more reason I make sure you get home safely."

"We're not babies," Simon pointed out. "I drive the tractor and ride our plow horse."

"I did those things when I was your age," Jeremiah replied, showing Simon how to throw out his line so he wouldn't get it tangled in the beams at the top of the arch. "But usually I had adults nearby." He waited a few beats, then asked, "So, Eli, does your *mamm* even know you're gone?"

Eli pulled in his line. "I told her we were going to check out the new baby lamb."

"So she thinks you're behind the barn back home."

"*Ja.* She's visiting with Simon's *mamm* in the kitchen. They can chatter for hours and never miss us."

Jeremiah glanced at the gloaming. He was wet and starting to chill but he couldn't go home yet. "So that means when we get there, you have to be honest with her, okay?"

"I can't. She'll punish me."

"Better to be honest and take the punishment now than to hold a lie in your heart."

"What about me?" Simon asked with big brown eyes. "Can I just hold the lie in my heart?"

Jeremiah shook his head. "No, you are to go back to Eli's house with me and then face your own *mamm*."

"And then I'll get in trouble, too."

"You're both already in trouble," Jeremiah said, wondering how much trouble he'd get into because of this. "But as infractions go, fishing isn't such a bad one."

"What's an infraction?" Simon asked as they rolled up their lines, fishing forgotten now.

"I think it means when we don't obey our parents...or anyone else," Eli added, staring at Jeremiah. Then he asked, "Did you get infracted a lot when you went away and shot people?"

Jeremiah didn't know how to answer that, but he went with the truth and left out the details. "Most people get in trouble now and then. I've had my fair share."

"Did you confess and take your punishment?" Eli asked, his eyes burning with the need to know.

"I did," Jeremiah replied. "We have to be men about these things. Take it and get on with life. Learn from our mistakes." Then he stopped as they came off the bridge. "I'm dealing with a big infraction right now because I left, but when I get baptized, I'll be forgiven and I won't have to worry about that again."

"You're kind of old for that," Simon pointed out.

"Never too old to turn my life over to God.

I'm catching up and once it's done, I'll never leave again."

"Then can you take us fishing for real?" Eli asked, hopeful.

Jeremiah laughed and nodded. "Then, yes, we'll go fishing at a decent time of day and with the proper equipment and bait and *with permission*, for real. But right now, I need to get you two home so your mamas won't be worried."

"And to face our fate," Simon said in a somber tone.

"*Ja*, and my own, too," Jeremiah replied. He had a feeling that when Ava Jane saw him with the boys, it wouldn't go over very well.

Ava Jane laughed at another of Ruth Kemp's funny stories. Ruth could take an ordinary event and embellish it to the point of making everyone laugh. She had a great wit and a comic streak that made her bubbly and happy all the time.

"Oh, look at the time," Ruth said, hopping off her chair. "I've sputtered on so long that you must be starving for your supper."

"We're having more leftovers," Ava Jane said. "But, yes, I need to round up the *kinder*." She could hear Sarah Rose upstairs with Ruth's daughter, Rebecca, laughing and playing with their rag dolls and other toys. But Eli and Simon had been quiet. Too quiet.

"I'll call the boys back in," Ruth said, heading to the kitchen door. But she stopped with her hand on the screen. "Oh, my."

"Was der letz?"

Ava Jane followed Ruth to the door and stared out into the golden dusk. Then she saw Jeremiah walking along with Eli and Simon, his clothes and hair wet, the boys carrying fishing poles.

Pushing past Ruth with a building fear and anger, she rushed toward the boys and Jeremiah. "What have you been up to?" she said, directing her anger toward Jeremiah. "Did you take them swimming without even consulting me? Jeremiah, how could you?"

Jeremiah stood silent, his expression a stone wall of regret and disappointment. Eli looked from her to Jeremiah. Simon hung his head.

"Will someone please explain?" Ava Jane said, her voice rising, her pulse hammering. She'd never be able to trust him. Why had she even tried?

"Simon?" Ruth called, her hand out to her son. *"Kumm* and tell me what happened."

Jeremiah didn't speak. Didn't move.

Ava Jane didn't ask again. Instead, she let loose on him. "You know how I feel about this and yet you somehow take them off and with it growing dark, too. I don't understand how a grown man—"

"He didn't do it, Mamm," Eli shouted over her rant, his expression muddled with an anxiousness she'd never seen before. "He didn't do anything wrong. Me and Simon... We sneaked away. We weren't playing with the lambs. We went fishing."

Ava Jane gulped a breath, her eyes slamming into Jeremiah's. She saw the truth in his silence.

Glancing from him to her son, she asked, "Eli, you did this all on your own?"

Eli squinted and toed the dirt with one muddy boot, his eyes downcast. "Yes, ma'am. Mr. Jeremiah had been swimming and he found us and told us we had to come home and tell the truth. So that's the truth. We have to own up and learn from our mistakes. He told us that, too." Lowering his head and adjusting his hat, he added, "We're sorry. Very sorry."

Simon bobbed his head. "We don't want to be infractioning again, ever." He glanced up at Jeremiah, admiration in his brown eyes. "Mr. Jeremiah said he'd teach us to fish, once he's baptized and forgiven, and if we get proper permission. Which we will, promise."

Ruth took Simon into her arms and then nodded toward Jeremiah before she lifted her son's chin with one hand. "*Denke* for being honest. We will discuss your punishment when we get home. Now, go and fetch your sister. We're leaving."

Simon nodded and took off.

Ruth turned back to Jeremiah. "*Denke* for watching out for the boys. Simon's father works long hours at a nearby lumberyard so he has little time to take the boy out fishing and hunting. I'm sorry for the inconvenience."

"No inconvenience," Jeremiah said, his eyes still on Ava Jane. "None at all."

Ava Jane's skin heated with a rush of regret and embarrassment. "Jeremiah…"

The other children came running out, the door's urgent slam causing Ava Jane to almost jump out of her skin.

"I'll talk to you later," Ruth said, before hurrying her children into their buggy.

Eli's gazed moved between Ava Jane and Jeremiah and then he took Sarah Rose by the hand and urged her into the house, ignoring her prattling and questions.

Ava Jane stood and watched to make sure they were out of earshot and then turned back to Jeremiah. "Can we talk?"

He didn't speak at first. He only stared at her, a hard frown marring his beautiful face. Then he shook his head. "You will never forgive me. You'll pretend to care and you'll even try to convince yourself that you've let the past go. But if you can't trust me, especially with your children, then what is there left for us to talk about, Ava Jane?"

He pivoted to leave, a dark silhouette against the blood-orange sunset.

And her heart went with him.

"Jeremiah," she called. "Please come back."

He kept walking, his broad shoulders slumped in defeat.

Ava Jane sank down on the steps and watched him until her eyes burned from the fading brilliance of a beautiful sky.

Chapter Eighteen

A couple of days later, Jeremiah sat with his father, silent and waiting for the right words. He couldn't forget the other night and the anger and condemnation in Ava Jane's eyes.

The community might be slowly accepting him and forgiving him, but the woman he loved never would. He'd fought with his team members against massive enemies and learned how to compartmentalize his feelings. But he'd never fought anything that hurt him more than losing Ava Jane.

"I remember Gideon," he finally said to Isaac. "With the army of three hundred against all of those thousands of Midianites. That's what my team and I were constantly up against—the kind of enemy that always has more coming. But just like Gideon and his men, we were trained to use our own form of trumpets and torches. To be more than we seemed. That way we could take them down, one by one, with the right strategy and detailed plans. And with a level of trust among us that brooked no questions." Stopping, he held his hands together. "I trusted the Lord during those times. Don't get why some had to die, but I never wavered on trusting the Lord."

He thought about how hard he'd worked since coming home to win trust, to receive forgiveness. A weariness settled over him, heavy like combat gear. He'd hoped Ava Jane would come around.

The other night she'd made it clear she might not be able to truly forgive him or trust him.

"I'm searching for that kind of trust now, Daed. I want others to trust me and I want to be able to trust in return. But I don't know if I'll ever have anyone's trust again."

Jeremiah ran a hand over his hair. He'd let it grow when he'd returned stateside. It was longer now, thick. Beth had trimmed it for him. Soon, he hoped to have a beard to match. A beard that would signify him as a married man.

"I have to keep fighting, keep waiting on the Lord. I have to overcome the enemy, the doubt and the fear. I have to trick the enemy and win the battle. I'll keep pressing against the rock of her resistance, holding it steady, until I win her heart again."

One step forward. Two steps back. He'd regroup and start over. But there might come the time he dreaded. The time he'd finally give up and walk away.

"The enemy is my own doubt and fear, telling me to leave again. To just go away and never return." Leaning in, he whispered, his eyes on his father, "But I won't be a coward. I won't put down my armor until this final battle is over. I came back for God. His grace is sufficient."

His father sighed in his sleep.

Jeremiah closed his eyes and said his morning prayers, the silence of a quiet echo covering him in God's warmth.

Then he looked at his father's gaunt, pale face and remembered the man he'd once been. Jeremiah turned and thought about the man *he'd* once been, too.

"I will be the man You need me to be, Father. I can do that, for You," he said as he looked upward.

He went into the kitchen and found some breakfast and headed out to do his day's work so he could keep his mind off the woman who had accused him of trying to lead her son astray.

Three hours into cleaning the barn, Jeremiah looked out the wide-open doors as he heard a buggy approaching the house.

His mother wasn't feeling well, so she was

resting this morning while Derek stayed near Isaac. Beth had decided at the last minute to go next door to a quilting frolic since he or Derek could reach her there if anything changed with their father. So he wasn't expecting anyone and he really didn't want to see anyone.

He was covered with dust and cobwebs, and probably smelled worse than a billy goat. He prayed this wasn't some well-meaning mother bringing around yet another daughter to gawk at him.

But he couldn't ignore anyone's kindness, especially if they'd come to check on his *daed* and bring food. Wiping at his brow and arms with a cleaning rag, Jeremiah walked out and waited by the barn doors.

Then he recognized the woman driving the small open buggy.

Ava Jane Graber.

Ava Jane saw Jeremiah emerge from the barn and wondered if he'd ignore her. But he didn't do that. Instead, he started walking toward her. He'd show courtesy to a woman, even a woman who'd been cruel in assuming the worst about him. But after a couple of sleepless nights and a lot of Bible reading and praying, she hoped she could make that up to him today.

"Ava Jane," he said by way of a greeting. His

rolled-up shirtsleeves showed off his impressive biceps while he wiped his face and hands with an old rag. "What are you doing here?"

Even though he was filthy and a dark scowl sat plastered across his face, he still made her heart jump too fast. *Swagger*, she reminded herself. That could get her in trouble.

She'd come here to apologize and make amends. Not stare at the man.

Hesitant now, she wished she'd thought this through a little more, but she straightened her spine as she started down out of the buggy. Jeremiah hurried to help her down and then stood back, stoic and still hurt from the look of the unyielding frown covering his face.

"I brought you some lunch," she said. "I thought we could visit for a spell."

She'd missed the quilting frolic because she wanted to talk to him. At the insistence of her coconspirator, Deborah, after she'd poured her heart out to Deborah a little while ago, they'd managed to coordinate this little excursion with sneaky precision. Beth was one farm over at the frolic. Deborah had convinced Beth to attend with her earlier today. And Moselle didn't want any visitors, also according to Deborah. Even if Moselle happened to see them out the window, Ava Jane figured Jeremiah's mother wouldn't interrupt them. So Ava Jane had to say a lot in a little amount of time.

He didn't move, so she turned to get the picnic basket she'd filled with chicken salad and chopped-ham sandwiches, boiled eggs and snickerdoodle cookies. She'd also brought a jug of fresh lemon-mint tea.

"I've got it," he finally said from behind her. Taking the basket before she could lift it, he held it and waited.

"I brought an old quilt. For us to sit on."

"Why don't you leave it and go?" he retorted. "I'll tell Mamm you brought food."

Ava Jane blinked back tears at his cold monotone response to her picnic idea. His eyes held a brittleness that she'd put there and his pulse throbbed a warning beat along his strong jawline.

"Jeremiah, I brought the food for you."

"Why?"

He wasn't making this easy. But then she had not made things easy for him since day one. Her turn to be strong and focused, as he'd taught her. "Because I wanted to apologize for assuming the worst. I was wrong."

He moved back a couple of feet, his stance softening. "Why is it that you *always* assume the worst when I'm around?"

"Can we sit and have a talk?" she asked. "A real talk?"

"Chatter all you want."

He pivoted with the basket, so she grabbed the quilt and headed toward the barn with him. Setting the basket down, he moved toward the old water pump and washed his face and hands and then did his best to damply comb his hair with his fingers.

Which only added to her attraction.

Then he turned to look at her. "So you want to talk to me now? After what you said last time you saw me?"

"Yes, I thought we'd decided to...be friends."

"*Ja*, I thought that, too. But you find fault with me at every turn, Ava Jane." When they reached the yard near the house, he turned and tugged the quilt out of her hand and motioned to a towering live oak. "I'll sit here with you. Derek, the nurse, is in with Daed and Mamm. He can see us out the window from the downstairs bedroom and, since he's twice my size and willing to help anyone in trouble, you can call out to him if you don't like the way I chew my food."

Offended and burning with embarrassment, Ava Jane nodded but refused to spar with him. "Okay, let's eat and then I'll let you get back to work. I have things to do myself today." Things she'd abandoned to come on this misguided attempt to fix what she'd messed up so badly.

He threw down the quilt and offered her his hand. Ava Jane took it for a brief moment and then settled across from him and passed him two sandwiches and an egg.

Her own appetite lost, Ava Jane looked out over the hills and valleys surrounding the creek. "This is a *gut* view you have here. I always did love this farm."

He chewed and drank. "I missed this place so much."

She heard the longing in his voice. "Jeremiah, I *am* sorry. I've been horrible to you and I keep making a mess of things, no matter how hard I pray to do better."

Putting down what used to be a sandwich and was now crumbs and a napkin, he stared out over the creek and hills with a scowl that took it's time turning soft. "I deserved your harsh treatment."

"No, what you deserve is my prayers and my hopes. It's always a celebration when someone is lost but returns home."

"Home. I missed that word and all it means to me."

She found the cookies and opened the container to place it between them. Just so she wouldn't reach out and push damp hair off his forehead. "Your home missed you. Your family missed you."

"Did *you* miss me, ever?"

"All the time." She could admit that now. It should hurt but it didn't. "I loved Jacob. He was a *gut* man, the best husband, and he loved me and our children."

"I believe that," Jeremiah said, turning to her, all traces of his anger gone now. "You'd be a devoted wife."

She nodded, tears forming again at the way he'd said that. Not *you were. You'd be.* "He courted me in a slow, gentle way and… I came to care about him very deeply. He never once asked about my feelings for you. Because he knew. He knew, Jeremiah."

"Knew what?"

She stilled, her heart beating so hard and fast she was sure Jeremiah could hear it. "That I still thought of you." She looked away and out over the distant water. "He thought about you a lot, too. It was like this unspoken rule, how we both thought about you but never talked about you."

Then the tears came because the guilt she'd held inside for so long now glared at her and, like the lesson Jeremiah had taught her son the other night, she knew she had to tell the truth.

"I… I didn't tell him enough that I loved him. I should have told him that…he was more than second best." Holding a hand to her lips, she said, "The day he died, I was angry that the calf had got out, that the fence hadn't been mended. He went after the calf because of me and I never stopped to think that anything bad could happen to him. I should have called after him or gone with him. I never got the chance to tell him I loved him. That he wasn't second best. He was *the* best."

Jeremiah's sharp intake of breath caused her to look his way. Silent tears streamed down his face. "Is this why you keep pushing me away, because you're punishing yourself instead of me? Or maybe as much as me?"

She couldn't speak. The acknowledgment of something she'd held inside for so long seemed to open the floodgates of her pain. Holding her hands in her lap, she lowered her head. "I should have loved him more."

Jeremiah reached across and took one of her hands in his. "And I should have never left you."

She shook her head. "My *daed* says there has to be some good in all of this. Maybe you had to leave in order to truly return."

He stared into her eyes, his heart revealed in the dark blue mist of his gaze. "I hope there is good. I want to find the good." His gaze moved over her face, his eyes going dark with a new raw emotion that left her longing and too aware of his closeness. "But, Ava Jane, you need to let go of that blame you've been holding for so long. You had no way of knowing what would happen that day. It's terrible and it hurts, I understand that. But it wasn't your fault. Let that go, okay?"

She took a breath, a great weight lifting off of her, releasing her. "I've never told anyone the truth, not even Deborah or Mamm." Her eyes holding his, she said, "You're the only one who can understand and, Jeremiah, on this I trust you. Only you."

He lifted his chin, his lips trembling. "I asked God to show me the way. You've trusted me with your deepest secret. I'll hold your words dear to my heart forever."

Jeremiah held tightly to her hand and nodded, too overcome to say much more. They sat that way for a while, their gazes on the ducks with new ducklings out in the creek and the birds that sang fresh songs through the trees.

Ava Jane felt a peace she hadn't felt in a long time. "I'm glad I came to see you today."

Jeremiah nodded and let go of her hand, then shot her a dazzling grin. He looked younger. "Me, too. I love snickerdoodles."

She laughed at that and handed him the rest of the food. "I have to go."

He got up with her. "I'm glad we're becoming friends again."

"*Ja*, me, too." She planned to trust him more from here on out. Hesitating, she said, "If you'd like, come to Sarah Rose's birthday party this Saturday. I made her a quilt and she'll have friends over. Maybe you could take her brother fishing so he won't antagonize the girls."

"Oh, so now I see the real reason you've plied me with food," he said, smiling.

Seeing the teasing gleam in his eyes, she relaxed. "I came to start over. Again." Then she shrugged. "But Eli needs to be doing more boy stuff. Daed tries but he's often tired. Eli seems to listen to you."

Jeremiah's eyes filled with humility. "I'm not a hero, Ava Jane. But I'd be honored to spend time with Eli. With all of you."

Ava Jane had to swallow the lump in her throat. "We're going to get through this, Jeremiah. With God's guidance."

When they heard female chattering coming up the lane in the front of the house, they parted and gathered up the lunch items.

"Deborah and Beth," he said. "*Gut* to hear them laughing together."

"Good to see you smiling," she said, meaning it. "I'll go and tell Beth hello and grab my sister, and I'll be on my way."

Jeremiah took the basket and the quilt. "I'll drop the quilt in the buggy and I'll bring the basket by later. You go on to them because you know they'll be curious."

At one time, Ava Jane would have run the other way. But she wasn't worried about assumptions anymore. On their part or hers.

"*Denke*, Jeremiah."

Giving him one last smile that came from her heart, she hurried to greet their giggling, curious sisters.

Chapter Nineteen

"This is an exciting day," Deborah said a few days later, standing in Ava Jane's fresh, clean kitchen. "Sarah Rose has grown so much in the last year. She's going to be as pretty as her *mamm*."

Ava Jane smiled at her sister and breathed in the fresh air from the open windows. "She's willful and stubborn but she's a *gut* girl."

"As I said, like her mother." Deborah checked the baked chicken with vegetables that they'd taken out of the stove to cool a bit and admired the strawberry cake with pink and white icing Ava Jane had made yesterday. "So Leah's bringing her two girls and Ruth will be here with Rebecca, right?"

Ava Jane nodded. "And two other girls her age. I also invited Jeremiah and Beth, too."

Deborah fluffed napkins and rearranged

flowers, her eyes full of so many questions. "Beth told me about that. So going to visit him helped smooth things over between the two of you?"

"I told you that the other day when you and Beth came back to her house. You know, the day you two cornered me on the porch and made me give you all the details of our picnic."

Remembering that day, Ava Jane grew warm inside. She and Jeremiah had connected that day. A small thread of trust had been woven between them. After telling him about her guilt and agony over what had happened the day Jacob died, Ava Jane's yoke of burden had lightened. Jeremiah's whole stance had softened, too. She could see that in the way he'd looked at her. She prayed they could hold together that fragile thread.

Deborah slapped at her wrist. "*Ja*, because we found the two of you looking mighty close and chummy."

"Friends, Deborah. We are friends," Ava Jane pointed out yet again. Her sister waffled on wanting them together and wishing they'd stay apart. "We have to start somewhere."

"I'm glad you two are friends," Deborah said with a little eye roll. "So what else needs to be done around here?"

Ava Jane checked the kitchen. "We have the baked chicken and vegetables, rice and gravy, salad and cake. Tea is made and lemonade is freshly squeezed. Mamm is in charge of the cookie table. The volleyball net is set up and the rubber ball and bat are out for baseball."

Deborah clapped her hands like a little kid. "And Daed and some of the men are out there arranging tables and chairs. Oh, look. There's Jeremiah."

Ava Jane whirled so quickly she knocked a cutting board off the table. Vegetable scraps went flying all over the clean floor. Mortified, she bent to grab the cutting board.

"Seeing your friend sure does make you jittery," her sister said with a saucy grin while she went about, gathering scraps. "I'll clean this up. You'd better go out there and supervise setting up those tables and chairs and maybe offer Jeremiah a cookie."

Ava Jane took a deep breath. "What was I thinking? I shouldn't have invited him. His father is so ill. He should be with him."

"He can be reached if anything happens with Ike," Deborah said. "Having him here to keep the boys occupied is a *gut* idea. And it will be a signal to others that it's time to really forgive him."

Ava Jane's pulse raced in waves of awareness once she reached the backyard. He looked nice in his fresh broadcloth pants and white shirt, his dark hair curling around his face and neck. Jeremiah didn't stand around. He went to work on moving chairs and tables so they'd be in the shade later this afternoon. Eli and Simon, who'd come on foot ahead of his parents, followed Jeremiah around like two puppies, eager to help and learn. He put them to work, guiding them on how to arrange the tables and put on cloths, the lines of each straight and crisp.

She'd worried about him being a bad influence on her children and here he was, being a good encouraging adult, after all.

I needed to change more than he did, Father.

Ignoring her fascinated sister's covert stares, she straightened her dress and apron and went out to finish setting up for the party. When she saw her mother also helping, Ava Jane relaxed and went to say hello.

"Mamm, I didn't know you were already out here working."

Her mother whirled from placing a giant tray full of oatmeal cookies on the table. "Your *daed* put me to work before I ever made it into the house." Hugging Ava Jane close, she said, "*Gut* day, daughter."

"It's a perfect day," Ava Jane said, the light breeze lifting her *kapp* ties. "I'm so glad you're here."

Mamm glanced at Jeremiah. "I see you've invited extra help."

"Yes, but Beth was supposed to come, too. Let me go and find out why she didn't."

Martha's eyebrows shot up. "You and Jeremiah—"

"Are on friendly terms now. He's here to distract the boys." She explained about Eli wanting to go fishing and how Jeremiah had brought the boys home the other night. "I had to quit fighting against that and let someone else who knows how to fish take over that task. He took care of them the other night and I am grateful for that."

"Smart idea," her mother said. "I'm glad you've found it in your heart to be kind to him since he seems to know how to handle rambunctious boys. Kindness costs you nothing."

"Oh, it cost a lot," Ava Jane retorted. "But it's also taught me a lot. God uses our suffering to teach us, doesn't He?"

"Yes, sometimes He does indeed do that." Her mother stared after her but didn't respond any further.

Ava Jane got the feeling that her family

had forgiven Jeremiah long before she'd even thought about doing so.

He looked up to find her coming toward him, a sight he'd often dreamed of but never hoped to witness again.

Seeing the tentative smile on her face, Jeremiah relaxed and hurried to meet Ava Jane. While he strolled toward her, he noticed her sparkling white apron and crisp blue dress. She was so pretty that it took his breath away. With each day, they moved closer to each other. He treasured these moments.

"Hello," he said, his hands at his side. Staying a respectable distance away, he added, "Is there something else I can do before the party starts?"

"No," Ava Jane said, checking the white cloths on the tables and the bounty of food being spread across the serving table. "We normally don't make big deals out of birthdays, but Sarah Rose is growing up and… I made her a special quilt. She misses her *daed* so much, I thought I'd pamper her this year. Now Eli will expect the same."

"I didn't know we could pamper each other," he said, half teasing. "It sounds nice."

"Every now and then," she replied. "And within reason."

He nodded. "So I have new fishing poles for

the boys and lots of bait—worms and crickets. But I will not pamper them, I promise. They have to learn to bait their own hooks and remove the fish when they catch them. Which they will do."

She laughed at his blustering confidence. "Well, you have to eat first. We have plenty of food. Can't go fishing on an empty stomach."

"Is that my payment then? A good meal?"

"Is that a good enough payment?"

He nodded. "Better than enough." Then he lowered his voice. "I'll take it for now anyway."

Giving him a surprised wide-eyed stare, she blushed and went to work straightening an already-straight tablecloth. Then she turned and said, "After you and the boys eat, you can go ahead and take them fishing. We have games for the girls and then I'll give Sarah Rose her quilt."

He'd flirted and now she was in a huff. *Way to go, Amish.*

Out in the world, his buddies had taught him how to flirt and sometimes things like what he'd just said still slipped out.

"Ava Jane?"

She rearranged the flowers in the center of the table. For the third time. *"Ja?"*

"I didn't mean to sound disrespectful. I appreciate the meal and the chance to see you and go fishing with the boys. I won't linger long. I want to check on Daed, as I do every night."

Understanding filled her eyes. And regret. "I shouldn't have asked you here. You need to be with your father as much as possible."

"I don't mind," he said, thinking he was botching this whole thing. "Mamm wanted Beth to come, too. But Mamm's had a cold all week and Beth decided to stay there with her. She's so tired these days."

"I'll miss seeing Beth and I hope your mother will feel better soon. Thank you for coming. We will send them some food."

Relieved, he asked, "So, we're...still friends?"

She shot him a confused glance. "*Ja*, I thought we'd settled that."

"But my teasing and flirting just now—"

"Was funny and...confusing," she admitted. "I'm going to ignore it. But I'll be glad to cook you meals now and then. How's that?"

"That works," he said with a grin. "I never turn down a meal from a friend."

Ava Jane glanced around, taking in all the people who'd come to help her celebrate Sarah Rose's birthday. Some would frown on making a fuss but this was like any other gathering, full of good fellowship and food, celebrating life and love. Sarah Rose and her friends were done with food and gifts and playing volleyball and baseball. They'd wandered toward the barns, probably to find a corner to chatter away in. Ava Jane's friends and family had insisted she sit and take a rest while they tidied things up in the kitchen. But she suspected all of the well-meaning matchmakers in her life hoped Jeremiah would come back and they'd have some quiet time together. She'd give them a few minutes to stew in their hope and then she'd clean her own kitchen, thank you.

She thought of Jeremiah and how she'd treated him with her high and mighty notions on how he should conduct his life. She still did not understand why he'd left and gone off to fight, but she could clearly see the warrior inside of him. It showed in his fierce need to do what was right, to be kind to others, to work hard to prove himself every day. Whatever influences had caused him to leave had been beyond her control. And maybe his, too. But God knew his heart. God had brought him home.

That was a cause for celebration. But her own bitterness had held her back from seeing that until now.

Things would be different now. She'd be kind to him. She'd visit his family more often and help them during this difficult time. She'd pray for him with a new spirit. Her emotions couldn't reach past that to anything more right now, even if her imagination had taken flight on too many what-ifs.

"You're sure in deep thought."

She looked up to see her *daed* smiling down at her. "I was counting my blessings," she said, searching the yard. "Where are the girls?"

"They ran off to check on the baby chicks and pick wildflowers out in the meadow," he said, sitting down beside her. "Sarah Rose sure did like the rose-patterned quilt you made for her."

Ava Jane glanced at the table where the quilt lay spread out in all of its glory, along with some books and a few other handmade items others had brought—dolls and shawls, a new bonnet. "She seemed glad, yes. I hope she will cherish it for a long time."

"I think she will," her father replied. "You seem happier today, daughter. More at peace."

"I am at peace," she said. "I have much to be at peace about. A *gut* life—one that I couldn't see for a while there."

"You and Jeremiah are getting along better?"

"Yes. We're friends. I want to put the past behind us."

"That's wonderful to my ears," her father said. "He has a couple more months before he is baptized. I believe he is sincere and he's ready to return to the fold."

"I'm glad to hear that and I believe that now, too," she replied. Getting up, she said, "I think I should go inside and see if Deborah has rearranged my whole kitchen."

Daed laughed at that. "That girl has a mind of her own."

Ava Jane started up the steps and then turned. "Will you check on the girls?" A memory of Eli telling her he'd be in the barn and winding up at the creek instead caused her heart to stop for a minute.

"On it," her *daed* replied. "They are as quiet as little mice, aren't they?"

"Too quiet," she said, a trace of worry clouding her peaceful mood.

Jeremiah helped Eli reel in the big bream, happy to see the boy's wide grin. "That's a fine one, Eli," he said. "And the third one you've caught."

"And Simon has two," Eli reminded him, sharing the bounty. The boy expertly held the flapping fish tight and removed the hook from his mouth. "I love fishing, Mr. Jeremiah."

"Well, you are good at it and we have a nice mess of bream," Jeremiah replied, his heart welling when he remembered fishing right here with Jacob. "We'll need to head home soon, but maybe a couple more casts."

The boys baited their hooks like pros and studied the water with the patience of Job for the next few minutes. Then they heard giggling and splashing around the bend, out in the wider part of the creek.

"Who is that?" Simon asked, craning his neck to see. Then he whirled toward Jeremiah. "That's my sister, Rebecca, and Sarah Rose, with their friends."

Jeremiah put down his pole and hurried to the other side of the bridge. "Sure is. How did they wind up down here?"

Eli came running, too. "I don't think Mamm would allow this. You know how she feels about us getting near the water."

"I don't like it either," Jeremiah said, concern filling his heart when he saw the girls wading in the shallows. The creek had a sharp drop-off in the middle.

"Should I go and get Mamm?" Eli asked.

"Not yet," Jeremiah replied. "But we're going down there to fetch them."

Leaving their poles and tackle box, they hurried off the bridge and rounded the path that ran by this part of the creek. Jeremiah searched and easily spotted the girls. "Hurry, boys." He called out, "Sarah Rose, Rebecca!"

But the chattering, splashing girls didn't hear him.

He called again. "Girls, come out of the water!"

Rebecca turned around and stepped toward the shore where the other girls were standing with their feet in the water.

Then he watched in horror as Sarah Rose took another step. Rebecca called her name. Sarah Rose looked around, stumbled.

And disappeared into the water.

Chapter Twenty

Jeremiah went into action, untying his boots as he ran. "Eli, run and get help. Tell one of the adults to go to the phone booth and call 9-1-1 for help, okay?" He looked back as he called out. "Simon, stay on the shore with the other girls. Don't leave them and don't let them get in the water."

"Yessir." Simon ran behind him while Eli took off in the other direction.

Jeremiah ripped off his boots and socks and headed into the water. He had to find Sarah Rose.

A few minutes after she'd sent her father to check on the girls, Ava Jane wiped the kitchen table and turned to smile at Leah, Ruth and Deborah. "We are finished. Now we can go and sit under the oak tree and have some lemonade.

Denke for the help. And thank you for coming to share in Sarah Rose's special day."

Mamm came in from the porch, carrying what was left of the cake. "The men are full and resting and your *daed* is still with the girls apparently. I saved Jeremiah a piece of this, and there is a plate on the stove for him to take home to Beth and Moselle."

Ava Jane smiled as she put a cover over the cake. Then she glanced outside. Jeremiah and the boys had wolfed down their food and left in a rush to get to the creek. "They should be back by now. Of course, if they're catching fish—"

Then she heard a shout. "Mamm! Mamm, hurry!"

Eli!

Pushing past the other women, she ran out the door and down the steps to where the men were gathering. "Eli, what is it? Where are Simon and Jeremiah?"

Daed hurried from the far side of the barn. "I can't find the girls."

Eli whirled to his grandfather. "They are all at the creek!" Then he ran to Ava Jane and buried his head in her apron. "We saw them and…they were in the water…and Sarah Rose—"

"What?" Ava Jane's heart stopped cold, a sick dread piercing the center of her being. "What?"

Eli's words came out in a breathless rush, his

eyes red rimmed and wide. "She fell in. Jeremiah went in after her. He said call for help."

Ava Jane gasped and then she ran. Ran as fast as she could to the creek, her mind whirling with memories of another day and another horrible memory. *No, no!* her heart shouted while she couldn't find her next breath. *Not my baby. Not sweet Sarah Rose.*

Jeremiah had to help her. He had to save her little girl.

Weariness tugged at his body. The weight of the cold water covered him and forced him to remember being in underwater training, cold and tired and weighed down with dive gear and tactical gear, praying he'd make it to the top again. Only today, he wasn't wearing the armor of war. Today, his own failures and shortcomings were weighing him down. He only had a few more precious seconds. He could stay down here and let the weight take him away, but he had a reason for being here. He had so much to be thankful for, to hope for.

And he had to find Sarah Rose. The precious seconds belonged to her, not him. He was trained and equipped but he only needed one weapon right now. The armor of God.

Help me, Father. Give me the strength. I have failed everyone but I will not break Ava Jane's heart again. And I will not go against Your word again.

He went to the bottom of the sharp drop-off, about eight feet deep here, and tried to see through the murky depths, tried to focus and remember his training. He might have to try another spot, but she'd stepped off right here. She had to be near.

He turned, treaded, watched. Waited.

And then he saw a little dress billowing up like a blossoming flower, a bonnet wet and pulling at her beautiful face.

Jeremiah swam as hard as he could and grabbed the little girl into his arms and pushed up, up, toward the last of the sun's brilliant rays. He surfaced and took a deep, cleansing breath and then he swam until he could touch the bottom and run through the muck holding him back. Pushing at her bonnet, he managed to get her head up so he could start mouth-to-mouth.

Holding Sarah Rose close, he noted her closed eyes and the blue around her lips. Then he felt her neck.

A pulse. She still had a pulse. He wouldn't have to do cardiac compressions. Yet.

Quickly laying her down on the grass and leaves near the shore, he flipped her on her stomach to clear her lungs of water. When that didn't revive her, he turned her onto her back.

Gulping air, Jeremiah told the others, "Stay back. I have to help her. I'm going to breathe into her mouth."

The girls cried and clutched each other.

Simon knelt beside him. "Should I help?"

Jeremiah looked up at the frightened boy. "No, keep the girls calm."

Then he went into combat mode and tried with all his might to save this life. This one life.

To make up for what he'd done out there.

To make up for what he'd done to Ava Jane.

To redeem himself at last and give his heart completely to God.

She saw him leaning over her child. A scream caught in her throat, a dark claw shredded her heart into little pieces.

"Sarah Rose!" she cried out. "Sarah Rose?"

Eli was right behind her, calling to her. But Ava Jane kept running, the sound of other voices echoing through the woods, the sound of a siren somewhere off in the distance.

"Jeremiah!" she called as she fell down beside Sarah Rose and tried to push him away. "Jeremiah, give me my child!"

"He's helping her," Simon said, grabbing Ava Jane's arm. "He knows what to do."

The boy's words halted her and she stared through her tears at the man trying to revive her daughter. Jeremiah methodically and carefully breathed air back into Sarah Rose's still little body and pumped at her chest, trying to save her life.

Ava Jane put her hands together. "Jeremiah, don't let her die. Please don't let her die."

He never looked up, never responded. He just kept doing what he had to do, stopping to check her breath and her pulse and then starting all over again, his strong hands so big and yet so gentle.

Eli sank down beside Ava Jane, his breath coming in great huffs. "Mamm, I thought she might be cold."

Ava Jane turned to see the rose-patterned quilt in her son's hands and realized he'd run home to get it. Grabbing Eli and hugging him close, she rocked him there and then held to the quilt. They'd had such a sweet, beautiful day. Surely God wouldn't let it end in such a tragedy.

"Denke," she managed to say, tears streaming down her face. *"Denke."*

A silence fell over the woods. The birds hushed. The air held still. Ava Jane heard others come up behind her, felt someone touching her arm. But she held to the quilt and watched Jeremiah fight a battle, his face lined with fatigue and despair. And she could see it all there in the shadows around his eyes, in the pallor of his skin. He'd suffered out there. But here, right now, all of his torment had come back to war with him. If Sarah Rose died, he'd never recover.

And neither would Ava Jane.

She held her hands together and prayed.

Then she noticed others bowing their heads. Her parents, her sister, their friends, the children. They all seemed to be praying. While the one man she had not wanted near her children kept working, breathing, touching, whispering words of encouragement to her daughter.

He finally stopped and looked up and over at Ava Jane, a dark torment coloring his eyes, a single gruff sob escaping from his mouth. Touching three fingers to Sarah Rose's neck, he tried to speak.

And then they all heard it—a cough, a moan. Water came out of Sarah Rose's mouth. Her eyes flew open and she coughed again, causing a collective cry of joy to fill the gloaming.

Ava Jane heard a weak cry. "Mamm?"

Jeremiah fell back on his knees, exhaustion overtaking him.

Ava Jane lifted and then dropped down beside her daughter and wrapped the quilt over her trembling little body. "I'm here," she said. "I'm here. Help is on the way."

Hugging her scared, confused daughter close,

Ava Jane looked up at Jeremiah, her eyes holding his, the love in her heart bursting forth at last. She'd always loved him. Now she knew she was *supposed* to love him. Later, she'd tell him her true feelings and make him see that he was worthy of so much more than her love alone.

So she gazed at him, gratitude in her heart, love in her soul, and prayed he'd see the truth.

He nodded at her, his eyes full of regret, and then got up and walked away.

Jeremiah needed to escape. He couldn't breathe, couldn't think. Everything he'd been through had erupted in those few minutes between finding Sarah Rose in the water and hearing her call out for her mother again. Now his life was all out there for him to see: the mistakes, the victories, the regret and the hope. His heart held too much weight, too much agony. The flashbacks came in great, shattering waves that blinded him.

Ava Jane's eyes had filled with gratitude and understanding and, instead of running to her, he'd walked away. He had to find a quiet spot and think things through. He couldn't accept her gratitude.

He wanted her love.

"Mr. Jeremiah?"

Jeremiah turned away from the lane that

would take him home and saw Eli standing there. He couldn't run from the boy.

Eli stared up at him with dark, brooding eyes. "*Denke* for saving my sister."

Jeremiah held tightly to his tears and nodded down at the boy.

"Hey, I hear you're the one who rescued the girl?"

The paramedic hurried up to Jeremiah and shook his hand. "Good job. Her vitals are stable and she's alert. She should be fine but we're taking her to the hospital for overnight observation and to make sure her lungs are clear. Good thing you knew CPR, man."

Jeremiah still couldn't speak.

Eli gave him an admiring stare and told the paramedic, "He…he was trained that way."

Then Eli ran off to be with his mother and sister while the paramedic's eyes filled with realization. Shaking Jeremiah's hand again, he said, "Welcome home."

Ava Jane sat in the hospital room that night, watching her daughter sleep. Deborah was on the small settee by the window, sleeping under a white blanket. Sarah Rose's quilt lay over the bedding, keeping her warm. She had not let go of it since Ava Jane had wrapped her in it.

She'd sent her parents home with Eli, telling them to come back tomorrow. They'd all be home tomorrow, she hoped.

She had to see Jeremiah. To thank him and tell him how she felt. He had to know that she loved him. Why had it taken something so tragic to make her admit that to herself?

He'd left, disappeared while everyone clustered around Sarah Rose to wish her well. The ambulance had carried Sarah Rose and Ava Jane off, with Daed promising they'd call a cab to get them to the hospital.

Ava Jane had glanced around, hoping to see Jeremiah so she could thank him. But he was nowhere to be found.

Chapter Twenty-One

He went to his father's side.

Jeremiah fell onto the chair and lowered his head.

"I... I need to talk to you, Daed."

It was late and his mother and sister were both asleep.

He'd walked until the moonlight covered him in shadows, until his wet clothes had turned to damp. Until the weariness crushing his soul had brought him home.

But he couldn't sleep. So he sat here and talked to his father. "I saved Sarah Rose tonight. She fell into the creek and almost drowned. Just like Jacob." He stopped, wiped at his eyes, took in a breath. "Just like me, Daed. I almost drowned in my own pain and sorrow. Funny how I could spend well over eighteen weeks training to become a SEAL and yet these last months of retraining myself to become Amish again have become the hardest test of my life. I still have some lessons to learn."

He sighed and laid his head in his hands on the bed. Prayers rattled through his head like tanks moving through a blown-up village. "I couldn't save them," he finally said. "Two children. Two little children who got caught in the cross fire. I lost Cowboy and Gator, I told you that. But I've never talked about the two little children. Villagers trying to get away. Somehow they'd got separated from their family and they got shot. I didn't shoot them but I tried to save them."

He stopped, his head down, tears soaking the blanket, the memory of those precious little faces so clear he could almost touch them. "The fear in their eyes, their cries, those things stay with me. Always."

Jeremiah's hands clutched the blanket. "I wanted to go back for them. I turned to run back and get them." And then another round of shots and he'd woken up in a hospital in Germany and refused to let anyone get in touch with his family. He had wanted to go back to sleep and never wake.

"I didn't save them. They told me I couldn't have saved them. That I almost died trying."

He remembered one of his buddies calling him. "Amish, you go home and start your life over. You did the best you could, man. You saved five of us. That counts for something."

"But I didn't save all of you," he'd replied.

Jeremiah kept his head down, confessing all now.

"Tonight, in that creek, I saw those innocent faces all over again. I could not have lived with myself if I'd failed Sarah Rose," he said to his father.

He lifted his head and wiped his eyes. Then he lowered his head again and sat silent, his prayers lifting up to God. He needed peace. He needed love. He needed forgiveness.

Jeremiah must have fallen asleep. For how long, he wasn't sure. But when he felt a hand on his head, he came awake and sat up to find his father's eyes on him.

"Daadi?"

Isaac's hand slipped down Jeremiah's arm. Jeremiah took his father's hand and held it, a soft, warm joy washing over his body. "I'm sorry, Daed."

Isaac nodded, a single tear moving down his skeletal face. Then, still holding Jeremiah's hand, he closed his eyes and took his last breath.

* * *

When Ava Jane and her parents brought Sarah Rose home the next afternoon, she was surprised to find a car waiting in her yard. A big black fancy car.

After they all unloaded and entered the house, her *daed* carrying a still-weak Sarah Rose, Deborah met them at the door.

"Who is here?" Ava Jane asked, wondering if someone from town had come to help out.

"It's me, dear."

Deborah turned and indicated the parlor.

Then Ava Jane saw her. Judy Campton sat in a high-backed chair, wearing a suit and pearls.

"How kind of you to come," Ava Jane said, turning to Judy. "If you let me get Sarah Rose situated, I'll be right back down."

Deborah shook her head. "Mamm and I will watch the *kinder*. You and Daed need to go with Mrs. Campton."

"Why?" Ava Jane asked, her heart too bruised to hear more bad news.

Judy Campton pushed off the chair. "Jeremiah's father died last night," she said. "And I'm afraid Jeremiah isn't taking it too well. I think he needs to see you."

Ava Jane whirled toward her parents.

"Go," Mamm said. "Sarah Rose will sleep

most of the day and Deborah and I will make sure she is taken care of. Eli, too."

"He'll need a minister," Daed said. "And I agree with Mrs. Campton. He probably needs a friend."

Ava Jane hugged Moselle and Beth close. "I'm so sorry for your loss."

They both nodded and thanked her while Daed stood with the bishop and several other men. A few neighboring women worked the kitchen in a system as old as time. They knew funerals and weddings and births. They knew life and death and hurt and love.

She was one of them and right now Jeremiah needed her. The quick ride over had been quiet but now she needed to see him, to make sure he was all right.

Mrs. Campton had taken a spot in a comfortable chair, Bettye with her now since she seemed as tired as Ava Jane felt. She nodded to Ava Jane so Ava Jane went over to her.

"Where is Jeremiah?" Ava Jane asked.

"When they called me, he was out in the barn," Mrs. Campton said. "He didn't want to talk to me. I hope you can help him."

Ava Jane lifted her spine and went out the back door. The sun shone a creamy yellow light on the growing wheat in the field beyond the house and bounced off the tall silo behind the barn. But inside, the dark coolness contrasted sharply, the muted shadows causing her to blink.

The animals were out in the paddock, grazing. The big high barn was quiet.

"Jeremiah?"

"Ja?"

She heard him, felt him, ached for him. "Jeremiah, it's Ava Jane. Can I come back?"

"Yes."

Ava Jane followed the sound of his voice. But when she saw him, her heart tripped over itself to get to him. He sat huddled in a corner with his hands hiding his face, as if he'd tried to curl into a tight ball.

Sinking down beside him, she didn't flinch. Instead, she put her hands over his and forced them away from his face. "Jeremiah, I'm so sorry."

He held on to her hands, his red-rimmed eyes bright with something that broke her and scared her. Such a raw pain, she wanted to turn away. But she didn't.

"He touched me," he said, his eyes widening now. "My *daed* touched me, Ava Jane."

She leaned against the wall, her hands still holding his. "You were with him last night?"

Bobbing his head, he said, *"Ja.* Early this morning, really. I talked to him the way I always do. Told him about my life as a SEAL. The training, the doubts, what we all had to endure."

Swallowing, he looked away through a crack of light pushing through the ceiling beams. "I told him about the children. A girl and a boy. Dark haired and olive skinned. They…got separated from their family and they cried out. I heard them and turned. I had tried to save Cowboy and Gator, two of my teammates. But I could not get to the children. I tried and then there was a blast and shots fired and… I couldn't save them."

Ava Jane gasped and held tightly when he tried to pull away. This was what Mrs. Campton had seen and had warned her about. He carried this with him, all the time. What must have he gone through when he'd gone into that water to save her child?

She tried to form the right words, but he started talking again. "It all came back. Leaving you, training, fighting, killing. When I went into that water, it all came pouring back over me. I wanted to stay down there, safe and covered and washed clean, but I had to save Sarah Rose. You know, to balance what I'd done, to appease those I couldn't save." Shifting, he touched a hand to her face. "I had to get back to you. But I needed to get back to God."

Ava Jane's heart burst with love and pride. "Jeremiah, I'm here. I'm here. You found me again."

"But I want you to love me. And if what I saw in your eyes was just gratitude—"

"Yes, gratitude," she said, never letting his hands slip away from hers. "But more than gratitude. I saw it all, too, Jeremiah. If you hadn't come home, Sarah Rose might have died last night."

"But if I'd never left—"

She shook her head. "*Ne*, we can't say what would have happened if you'd stayed. We can't know God's will for us. But I do know that my daughter is alive and well today because of you, and that my son walks taller now and wants to do right by people, and that many of the people of our community have seen you in action, running toward the hard things that most people run from. That is who you are, Jeremiah. That is who you have always been. And that is what I love about you."

He moved away. "I don't deserve your love, but I want it. I so want it."

She wasn't afraid now. Ava Jane moved in front of him and pulled his head up with her hands. "I love you. I always loved you but I loved Jacob, too. He's gone and he'd want you and me together. He'd understand. Your *daed* is gone but he forgave you, Jeremiah. He loved you. Don't push me away out of a sense of duty. Don't shut me out. Let me help you. Let me love you and give you that peace you seek." Kissing his tears again, she began to cry but through her tears she whispered, "Jeremiah, listen to me. I love you."

He stopped fighting against her and looked into her eyes. And then he pulled her close and shed all of the tears he'd held at bay for so long.

"I love you, too," he said, lifting his head to smile up at her. "And I'm going to prove that to you for the rest of my life."

One year later

Jeremiah walked into the parlor after doing the evening chores and found his wife asleep in her favorite rocking chair. He still couldn't believe that last fall Ava Jane had become his wife. She'd been so beautiful, walking toward him in the late-afternoon sunshine. He'd been so happy that day and he was even happier this evening.

Mrs. Campton had helped him find counseling and Ava Jane had waited for him to come back to her, but she'd also visited him and brought the children to see him.

"We'll be right here, when you are ready," she'd told him.

Now he'd been baptized and his beard was long. He was a married man. A happily married man.

When the nightmares tried to come, Ava Jane was there beside him. Mrs. Campton was always nearby. And the community stood solidly with him. He stayed busy teaching children to swim, and he still volunteered with the local fire department, farmed the land and did carpentry work on the side, while his amazing wife cooked and baked and gained a reputation for her wonderful cakes and muffins.

Now here he was, ready to rest at the end of the day, loving the beautiful routine of this quiet place that held his heart.

And now smiling at his beautiful wife.

As if sensing that, she opened her eyes and smiled back. "*Gut* evening, husband. You caught me taking a catnap."

"*Gut* evening, wife," he replied, kneeling to place a hand on her growing tummy. "I've been thinking. If it's a boy, we should name him Jacob."

Her eyes misty, she stared over at him. "Jacob Jeremiah Weaver. We can nickname him JJ."

"That's different," he said with a grin as the sunset washed over them in shades of burnished gold.

Slapping at his hand, she stood and tugged him close. "*Ja*, but then…so are we."

She was right about that. Different but the same. Because now God's light shone on their lives and brought the kind of warmth that sealed a man's soul.

Jeremiah Weaver, the Amish, was home at last.

* * * * *

If you loved this romantic story,
be sure to check out Lenora Worth's
other books:

HER LAKESIDE FAMILY
LAKESIDE SWEETHEART
LAKESIDE HERO
BAYOU SWEETHEART

Available now from Love Inspired!

Find more great reads at
www.LoveInspired.com

Dear Reader,

I did not set out to write an Amish story, but this idea came to me when I'd tried other ideas that didn't seem to be coming together. My husband took me for a walk on the beach and I saw it in my head. I saw Jeremiah in my head, walking toward home.

When I told the idea to my husband, he asked, "Is that a thing?"

And I said, "It could be a thing. It could be a story."

And so that is how a retired Navy SEAL returned to the community he'd left behind and found redemption and forgiveness with the people who took him back and gave him shelter. It was not an easy journey for Jeremiah and this was not an easy journey for me. But in the end, this story healed both of us.

I hope you enjoyed Jeremiah's story and I hope that it helped you in some way on your own faith journey. I plan to write more about Campton Creek and the Amish community that has become a part of my heart. God allowed me to stumble my way into the world of the Amish and I will do my best to honor that.

Until next time, may the angels watch over you. Always.

Lenora Worth

Get 2 Free Books,
<u>Plus</u> 2 Free Gifts—
just for trying the *Reader Service!*

LIS17R3

HOME on the RANCH

YES! Please send me the **Home on the Ranch Collection** in Larger Print. This collection begins with 3 FREE books and 2 FREE gifts in the first shipment. Along with my 3 free books, I'll also get the next 4 books from the Home on the Ranch Collection, in LARGER PRINT, which I may either return and owe nothing, or keep for the low price of $5.24 U.S./ $5.89 CDN each plus $2.99 for shipping and handling per shipment*. If I decide to continue, about once a month for 8 months I will get 6 or 7 more books, but will only need to pay for 4. That means 2 or 3 books in every shipment will be FREE! If I decide to keep the entire collection, I'll have paid for only 32 books because 19 books are FREE! I understand that accepting the 3 free books and gifts places me under no obligation to buy anything. I can always return a shipment and cancel at any time. My free books and gifts are mine to keep no matter what I decide.

268 HCN 3760 468 HCN 3760

Name   (PLEASE PRINT)

Address   Apt. #

City   State/Prov.   Zip/Postal Code

Signature (if under 18, a parent or guardian must sign)

Mail to the **Reader Service**:

IN U.S.A.: P.O. Box 1867, Buffalo, NY. 14240-1867
IN CANADA: P.O. Box 609, Fort Erie, Ontario L2A 5X3

READERSERVICE.COM

Manage your account online!
- Review your order history
- Manage your payments
- Update your address

We've designed the Reader Service website just for you.

Enjoy all the features!
- Discover new series available to you, and read excerpts from any series.
- Respond to mailings and special monthly offers.
- Browse the Bonus Bucks catalog and online-only exculsives.
- Share your feedback.

Visit us at:
ReaderService.com

RS16R